ACTION KADABRA

SHINGLES, BOOK 33

DREW HAYES

Burning, hot white flashes roared down from the ceiling. This was the showstopper, the big finish, and the pyro had to reflect that. Action had spent days going over the placement of each spark-dispenser with the tech team, ensuring that the spectacle would enhance the final moments of his show, rather than detract from it.

Gripping the first chainsaw, blade still slick with red juice from the freshly sliced watermelon, a borderline gory method to show his audience that the danger was quite real, Action spun it up through the air, catching it a short while after, and sending it on the same journey once more, soon joined by the second chainsaw, and then a third.

In the audience, several people were paying their checks, and one kept frantically signaling for a refill before the curtain drew closed. Half-priced drinks were one of the show's main draws, drawing in more people than the magic act, as his boss liked to let him know at least weekly. Playing for a lukewarm crowd might not be ideal, but it was still a stage. A place to hone his act and craft, until he was ready to make another try for the big leagues.

Now juggling three active chainsaws, Action stepped away from the stage's front, moving toward center as he brought his airborne tools. The spinning metal reflected the sparks' light, creating a disco-like effect on the magician himself. Standing tall, with muscular arms exposed out the side of his tank top and a jaw square enough to eat toast without butter, Action Kadabra didn't share the same look as many professional magicians. Then again, his act wasn't quite like theirs either.

Without warning, the first pendulum swung from stage right, huge blade flashing in the falling sparks. Action didn't merely dodge, he pulled a standing backflip, not missing a beat with his deadly juggling. "Uh oh! Looks like the dark forces of magic are finally making their full assault. What do you think, folks? Can we triumph?"

One drunk woman near the back let out an enthusiastic whoop of support, and someone in a corner covered by shadow offered up actual applause. It was the most encouragement Action had gotten during a show all week, and he let it fuel him.

"That's right we can. Because I am Action Kadabra, the man with the magic of action!"

Right on cue, two more pendulums swept the stage, soon joined by the third, forcing Action into a sudden dance for his safety. Chainsaws in the air, giant blades swinging toward him, hot sparks raining from the ceiling, this was more akin to a death trap than a trick. Yet Action never lost a step, leaping over one pendulum, only to grab hold of the next, bringing him back into position just in time to catch a chainsaw inches from the ground and fling it skyward once more.

Getting properly positioned, Action prepared for the finale. All three pendulums swung in simultaneously, just as he gathered the three chainsaws in his hands at once, barely able to keep them all in grip. As the pendulums moved, he hurled the chainsaws up at once into a calculated arc, one that sent them back down in near perfect unison with the pendulums. Just as it seemed like Action would be skewered entirely, an extra-bright flash erupted from the pyro, momentarily blinding the audience.

By the time they'd cleared their eyes, there was a pileup of sharp objects in the center of the stage, seemingly covering Action entirely. It was only when the lights came on that they heard his voice once more, this time emanating from the rear of the room.

"Thank you, everyone. Thank you for your time, and your belief. I have been Action Kadabra, and we hope to see you again soon!" He was waiting by the rear exit, pen in hand just in case somebody wanted an autograph.

Some of the patrons gave him nods or warm smiles as they silently paraded past, minds already on the sounds of dropping coins and rolling dice only steps away. Working in an Off-Strip casino wasn't luxurious by any means, but they had a steady flow of customers, some of whom would occasionally become audience members. They were even nice every now and then, the drunk woman who Action believed hollered at him tucked five dollars into the top of his tank top. He thanked her and palmed the money, not in a position to turn down anyone's generosity.

The last patron of the night was unfamiliar—Action could usually note everyone's face from the stage thanks to the thin numbers—yet this fellow rang no bells. Not until he remembered the clapping from the shadowy area where several lightbulbs needed changing.

"You are quite talented." There was a slight tinge of accent to the man's voice, so far removed it was impossible to place, but otherwise he sounded unnervingly composed. "Strong, fast, excellent reaction times."

"Happy to hear you enjoyed the show. I'm here Monday through Thursday, and sometimes they let me help on weekends if our main act is busy." By "busy" Action really meant "too drunk to do card tricks," but that was more detail than a customer needed.

"With talent like yours, perhaps you'd be interested in something my employer is putting together. Very selective, we only choose sixteen people to compete each year."

Action raised a well-trimmed eyebrow. "And you hunt for that talent in rundown old casino shows?"

"We search anywhere we think someone might be underappreciated for their skills. I'd heard the rumors of what you could do; seeing it for myself was another matter." The man attempted to look sheepish, poorly, and added a bit of apology to his voice. "There is also the chance that we had a competitor drop out due to injury and have a sudden vacancy to fill."

Just as Action was about to wave the man on, the fellow reached into a suit jacket and produced a small envelope, handing it over. Curiosity won out over judgement, and Action partially opened the envelope to reveal a sudden stack of green. Eyes wide, Action jerked his eyes back to the strange man who was already smiling. "A first-class plane ticket, leaving tomorrow, to the port where you'll be sailing from, along with some spare cash for incidentals."

"Whoa, we haven't even agreed to anything yet. You aren't afraid I'll take this and keep it?"

"I have no concern over such trivial amounts. Compared to the five million dollars in prize money, that is a mere pittance, to say nothing of the lush food and accommodations awaiting our competitors."

At the word "food," Action's chiseled stomach let out an audible groan. Supporting that much muscle took a good chunk of protein, and he constantly felt like he was running on fumes. Chuckling at the noise, the stranger patted him on the shoulder. "I hope to see you there. With skills like yours, who knows how far you could go?"

"Hang on, you can't leave. We haven't talked details."

"You know all there is to convey at this juncture. If you have the courage, then the next step is clear. If not, enjoy the tip for a well-performed show." With that, the strange man stepped away from Action, back into the casino.

He didn't linger for long, however. Soon he was out a side door, ancient ring already on his hand, conjuring a portal back to the island. Filling in the ranks last-minute was never easy, which was why they kept a list of hard cases that would be desperate, just in case. Obviously some magician wouldn't do very well in a fighting tournament, but he looked the part enough to pass muster and fill out the last slot. It was really all about the big final anyway; so long as that delivered, Sorsero and Scrabraz would both be happy and the cannon fodder entrants like Action wouldn't matter.

After the first round, he'd just be one more corpse on the pile.

2

Action looked over the location once more, just to be absolutely certain he was in the right spot. This was the dock, and there was the pier, but no boat to speak of. If not for the bustle of staff clearly preparing for one to arrive, he might have suspected this all to be some ridiculous joke. Even if that were the case, however, he'd managed to pocket over half the travel money by packing himself into tiny seats. The notion of an action-magician wasn't one that took instant hold with many people. Every dollar he could save let him keep the dream alive for a few weeks longer.

A chill blew in across the dark ocean, lit only by a nearly full moon peeking out from behind the clouds. Action shivered, scanning around for a warm place to wait. He was over an hour early, but late to a boat wasn't a risk he'd wanted to take. Not with the kind of money promised on the line. Flashes of neon caught his eye. A bar named Scuttle was just past the edge of the docks, strains of music drifting along through the air. It had a seedy veneer; however, a fresh gust of wind forced Action's hand. While he'd worn a hoodie over his tank top, this was a job for a much thicker coat.

In no time, he was walking through the doors, greeted by a wave of heat more from the crush of bodies than the struggling AC system. It was shocking how *full* a bar like this was, especially in the middle of the night. The shock was short-lived as Action got a better look of the room and all the people in it. There was a guy dressed like a cowboy, another whose ensemble revolved around flames, someone clad in a full pinstripe suit, not to mention a woman holding a prop sword that ran nearly the length of her body.

Right, *of course* there would be other acts present. This was a competition, after all, and one willing to invite an act like him. Action had no idea how many were fellow magicians, or if their acts were more Avant Garde. He slunk away toward the bar, sticking to the edges of the room as he assessed those he would be up against. The large trunk slunk on Action's back contained most of his act, short of the installed features like pyro and pendulums, not to mention a few tricks he'd been working on. Whether or not he'd have to dig into the prototypes was a matter of how good these others were, but he hoped it didn't come to that. So far, the results hadn't exactly been consistent. Or safe.

"You sap-sucking-sons-of-shits!" With his focus so intently on the room as a whole, Action hadn't realized he nearly side-stepped on top of someone. The almost mistake was even less forgivable considering the size of the man, a huge fellow in red and black plaid. His beard and hair were fused beyond parting, giving his whole head the appearance of a furry alien with small openings for eyes and a cursing mouth. "This isn't how axes work."

Backpedaling quickly, Action realized the fury wasn't aimed at him. In fact, despite how close he'd gotten, the stranger didn't even appear to have noticed their near impact. All attention was on the arcade cabinet he was slapping at, furiously attempting to kill the most woodpeckers on an old Lumber Lord game. A series of tones signifying death rang out, and for a moment the man's hand dipped toward a huge duffel slung over his shoulder, before the fingers curled into a fist.

"Nuh uh, you aren't winning that easy. I'll crack that honeycomb yet." Hands went to his side, patting for change that evidently wasn't present.

From his own pocket, Action produced a quarter, setting it onto the counter. On the off chance this guy had clocked the almost collusion, a little diplomacy seemed in order. "On me. The trick for the honeycomb is to attack the far end of the branches, not where they meet the tree. Makes them shake more."

Instead of a simple thanks, Action was met with a furry-faced glower. "You think you're better than me?"

"Just played this before," he hurriedly explained.

The large man stepped back, motioning to the cabinet. "Let's see what you got then."

Action wasn't sure if he was competing with this man or proving the tactic actually worked, and which of those results was less likely to get him in a bar fight right before one of the biggest opportunities of his career. Ultimately, he decided to do as he'd suggested. At least he wouldn't come off as full of shit. Some of the throws were admittedly tough; however, even years since the last playing sessions didn't matter in the face of a magician's dexterity and hand-eye coordination. By the time the level was done, he'd successfully dislodged the honeycomb, frozen the woodpeckers, and earned entrance onto the next stage.

The fresh screen had barely loaded when the big man shoved his way back in, staring down at it with something akin to reverence. "Hot buttered flapjacks, you really did it." He took hold of the controls as the new stage started, and Action started walking toward the bar once more.

He made it all of five steps before the notes of electronic death sang from the cabinet, and another two before a thick arm fell over his shoulders. "That was impressive, I have to say. Name's Tim, Tim Burly, practitioner of Lumberjack-style. How's about I buy you a beer as thanks, and you can tell me more about those moves of yours?"

It didn't feel much like a question, as Action was herded over toward a nearly empty section of bar. The only person drinking there was a completely bald man, down to the eyebrows, who appeared to be sweating despite the relatively mild inner temperature. Tim aimed him right toward the new stranger, barking out a greeting as they moved. "Stang! I found us someone else to drink with, and he's got some chops."

The bald man winced at the voice, before sighing loudly and spinning on his stool. "Did he even bother to get your name?"

"It's Action. Action Kadabra." Ordinarily, he felt self-conscious using his stage name, but given the monikers these two were wielding, that was clearly the way to go. Besides, it wasn't as if his real name was much better.

"Well Action, I'm Stang, because even though there can be a singer and a wrestler named Sting, apparently adding one more to the pile conjured all sorts of lawsuits. Master of Jelly-style. Pull up a seat and tell us about yourself. Have to find some way to kill time until the boat arrives."

Catching the bartender's attention, Action nodded to one of the three taps present, earning a glass of draft with too much foam for his troubles. "Also a good chance for you to learn about the competition."

"Look at that, skills *and* a modicum of sense." Stang took a towel from the counter and wiped his glistening forehead. "You might just be good company after all."

3

As Action sipped on his foamy beer, he paid close attention to Stang and Tim giving him the rundown of the room. Evidently, this was a long-running competition, and while he was new to it, some of the others had reputations that preceded them.

"River Slayer is here. I heard she might show up this time. Think she's as good with that sword as they say?" Tim didn't seem especially unnerved by the concept, more excited as he stared at the woman with the huge sword. Action presumed she must put on an incredible show to be this well known.

"No, I'm sure she killed the spirit of a river and founded her Anabranch-style purely on hype." Stang was drinking White Russians with extra cream, taking unsettling slurps when he paused. "We've also got Tex Western and Don Ron. Pretty sure I see RLD trying to be covert with a ballcap and sunglasses. I don't recognize the guy in flames, or any of the three trying to hide in the corners." Stang nodded to three separate people who Action realized were working hard to go unnoticed. One wore a torn-up old cloak, another was bundled up like he planned to visit a tundra, and the third was clad in a very expensive designer jacket with the hood pulled over his face. "There's always a few."

"So you've done this before?" Action asked, desperate for any insight he could get into what they'd be facing.

That earned a laugh from Stang and Tim both. It was Tim who replied, after slapping the table hard enough to give it a new wobble. "Done this before? Look who's trying to butter our biscuits. No, we know all this from paying attention to the stories and rumors. Not many people come back for two bites at this apple, even out of the few who survive."

Opening his mouth, Action tried to ask what the hell *that* meant. Unfortunately, he timed his response just as an enormous boat horn blasted from outside, rendering all sound inside the bar meaningless. By the time Action uncovered his ears and looked up, most of the other patrons were shuffling up from their respective table, Tim and Stang included.

"Come on, that's our ride." Tim shook his huge duffel bag, eliciting a horrendous clatter, while Stang chugged down the rest of his drink.

For a moment, Action considered excusing himself, halted largely by the awareness that he needed information. Whatever this event was, it wouldn't do to know less than his competition, and these two seemed nice enough. A tad odd, but that was par for the course working in entertainment.

He followed the pair outside, their farther position meaning they were among the last to exit, and found the others were largely clustered up together near the door. Looking around the crush of bodies, Action realized the docks were no longer so deserted. Dozens of people in black uniforms were scattered across the perimeter, faces obscured by masks and presumably night-vision goggles. They were everywhere, near the roads, on rooftops, hunkering behind alleys. It was like a murder of crows that had stolen human forms, along with a healthy amount of weaponry.

One of their own stepped forward, the hiding figure in the designer jacket. Reaching up, he pulled down the hood to reveal thin, slicked down hair and watery, glistening eyes. The face stirred a memory in Action's mind, someone he'd seen when they looked less pathetic. Before he could figure out from where, the question got answered for him.

"Attention, my so-called competitors. I am indeed Steven Cage, star of screen and master of Hollywood-style. While our host has deemed all of you as necessary to our upcoming competition, I disagree that you all are of adequate skill-level to face me. Therefore, I've hired some private security to help with screening. Consider this a culling field: only the worthy shall compete."

He spun around, nearly toppling over as he fell off-balance, then started jogging toward the boat. After a few seconds, he slowed down, panting for air, and called out to the mercenaries still waiting on the sidelines. "Well? That's the cue. Kill them already!"

The next sound Action heard was not gunshots, as he might have expected. Instead, it was a wet splatter as he looked over to find the woman named River Slayer had not only drawn her tremendous sword, but used it to cut through the squad of goons nearest to them along with the car they were taking cover behind.

Action watched as they fell, human beings sliced through their centers with no warning or time to react, tumbling to pieces as red rushed along the ground. Holy shit. Holy *shit*. These people had *fantastic* special effects. This close, Action would swear the horrifying viscera before him was real. Was this some sort of opening act? He hadn't realized they'd need to improv.

River's attack was a sort of starting bell for the others, who scattered from their clumped-up position moments before the bullets did begin to fly, the soldiers who were lucky enough to have distance finally opening fire. Action was moving with the group, staying close behind Tim's bulk. This offered him a front-row seat to watching Tim reach into the loud duffel and produce several hand-axes, along with one that looked designed for chopping trees that could fight back. With barely a glance, Tim chucked several axes into the heads of firing soldiers, solidifying Action's surety that this was all a performance. Those were near-impossible throws in this kind of situation, especially the way he effortlessly split their skulls.

Although, the idea of "impossible" got a bit shaky as he watched one of the others, a man covered in the dirty old cloak, take several rounds of fire directly into the back. Trails of blood trickled out, and growls of what Action could only assume to be pain rumbled from the man, moments before he charged forward and leapt atop his attacker. The guttural, ripping sounds were as terrible as they were short-lived. It was a cool scene overall, though Action might have used fewer squibs to make it feel more believable. In reality, the dude would be a pasta strainer after that many bullets.

"Watch out!" Stang reach over, grabbing a mercenary by the neck moments before the shadowy stranger could plunge a knife into Tim's back. No sooner was contact made than the soldier spasmed, dropping to the ground in visible pain. Behind him, another goon was taking aim. On instinct, Action hurled one of his flash-smokes, a handheld custom creation that causes a huge burst of light and generous billow of white smoke when thrown. It was inspired by ninja movies, except Action's always seemed to come out a little too bright.

The sudden flare behind Stang ruined his attacker's aim, causing the shot to go wide. All around the area, other soldiers began staggering about, rubbing at their goggles.

Tim slapped Action heartily on the back, nearly toppling him over. "Nice thinking! You gave them an axe to the eyes."

"Um, guys…" Stang was less impressed by the trick, probably because he was staring at the actual, factual, tank that had pulled in between them and the boat's entrance ramp. It was old as hell and visibly rusting, but still a giant obstacle made of metal. Bullets tore forth from the mobile battalion, stopped soon after as they struck and bounced off of the nearest target: the mysterious padded figure from the bar. Still dressed in layers and layers, the unknown person stood there, shielding everyone else from bullets as they bore the brunt of the tank's wrath.

Just when Action was about to ask what the plan was, a streak of fire ripped through the night, slamming into the tank, and causing a tremendous explosion. Even from as far as he was, Action could feel the heat. It was a wonder the thickly covered stranger hadn't melted at that proximity. Somewhere in the night, a lone voice of triumph rang out.

"Rocket Launcher Dave!"

Action looked around to find that the others were largely cleaning up stragglers. The cowboy, Tex Western according to Stang, was dislodging his spur from the temple of a dead mercenary, and Don Ron was wiping blood off the violin case clutched in his arm. The guy in flames was standing near a few smoldering bodies, and River was walking past six piles of body parts that probably used to be people. In the distance, Steven Cage hopped aboard a dark helicopter, evidently electing not to share a boat with his fellow competitors. Had he thought for a moment any of this was real, Action would have been lost in panic.

As things stood, most of his focus was on how he was going to compete with these people. It would take one hell of an illusion to top some of their acts.

4

———————

Morning light drifted in through Action's window, waking him from a mildly hungover sleep. After making it onto the boat, Tim and Stang had insisted they toast to a successful warm-up, and Action hadn't wanted to be rude. Well, that was part of it. The rest was trying to learn more about these people and how they'd managed to pull off such incredible illusions seemingly by the seat of their pants. There was obviously preliminary information he was missing; some of those tricks must have been coordinated in advance. Luckily, his well-timed flash had blinded quite a few attackers and came off as intentional, so none of the others had caught onto his incompetence quite yet.

Stumbling up from where he was resting on a small cot, a size that matched the rest of his cabin, Action rubbed his dully aching skull. The trouble with using drinking as a way to ply information out of people was that the same act also damaged one's capacity for accurate recall. In other words, most of the night was a blur. Action was impressed. Given where he worked, social drinking was practically one of his stage skills, and the others had clearly put him through the paces. Brushing his teeth to try and scrub away the residual flavors, Action wiped down in the sink as best he could before heading outside.

His plan was to head for the galley, where the others would probably be either still drinking or soundly passed out. Instead, Action was nearly bowled over by Tim and Stang, both of whom were looking annoyingly awake for the evening they'd shared.

"Finished your morning training I take it?" Tim didn't bother waiting for a response. His arm was already around Action's shoulder, spinning him around to the other direction. "We couldn't wait either. I hear they've got a breakfast buffet set up."

Spinning around, Action's head swam from something mostly other than the hangover. While the gently rocking of the craft had concealed the truth, they were no longer on the sea. Behind him was a port to which they were tethered, connected to a huge island with a mountain range that appeared to have been carved into various arms and feet, like the mountains were launching a series of blows against the sky itself.

"Scrabraz Island, home of the tournament." Stang was staring up at the mountains too, though his was not an expression of wonder. More hunger, if anything. "They say every species that has ever lived still walks somewhere on this island."

"I heard there's a fountain that turns other metals into silver," Tim added.

"I heard once per month there's a storm where it rains stone lizards that attack you," Stang countered.

"Quarter." All eyes turned to the heavily padded figure nearby, the same one who had reflected untold bullets in the evening prior. Action really wanted to figure out how he'd pulled that one; squibs were one thing, that was on an entire other level. "The stone lizards fall once per quarter. You should all hurry, and don't overeat."

The mystery man tottered off, face still unseen beneath the layers and layers of clothing. That was all the encouragement Tim needed, and his bulk started forward, essentially dragging Action along in the current with Stang close nearby. They headed down the wooden plank following the other early risers as well as a tremendous amount of red décor.

Between the carpet, hanging banners flapping in the sea breeze, giant signs, and dozens of people all wearing identical face-obscuring uniforms, it would have been much harder to wander off path than stay true. In no time, the scent of sizzling meat hit Action's nose as they rounded a sand-dune to reveal a tremendous breakfast spread. Stacks of pancakes, waffles, and pastries from regions past Action's level of knowledge were all piled together, next to a row of every side-dish he could ask for and multitudes more. Chefs were working at prepared stations taking on custom orders, and already quite busy.

It seemed they were not the early risers Action had thought. Before him was a huge table, long and elegantly set despite the outdoor conditions. Exactly sixteen seats were present, a great many of them filled. He saw River, Tex, and the flame-guy from last night, as well as Don Ron near an omelet station. The guy in the dirty cloak was piling a plate high with various meats, while the fully covered fellow they'd followed was sitting without touching any food. There were also new faces, like a woman in a poufy chef's hat, or the guy who looked like he was trying to haul an entire munitions supply strapped to his body. The loud snap of jaws crushing down drew Action's attention to a huge alligator at the end of a pitifully thin leash, chomping down on a chicken thrown by the woman sitting next to him.

Whoever put this together sure managed to get a wide variety of acts. Action helped himself to a few slices of bacon aside from egg-whites and chicken. Keeping the action movie leanness didn't come without sacrifice; however, his body needed a little dopamine, and a couple bites of salted fat would help get him ready for whatever the day ahead held in store.

Just as Action was winding down on breakfast, the sound of a bell rang out. Instantly, the others froze, so Action did the same. From nowhere, a gust of sand blew up north of their table, blocking everything in it from view. When the sand died down, there was suddenly a raised chair sitting there... no, a throne. Seated atop it was a lean man with small, focused eyes. He took in the table before him, drawing a razor-thin smile across his face.

"Greetings to all of you. My competitors, my challengers, my entertainment. I am Sorsero, the famed master of Enchantment-style, the parchment panther, former champion, and current master of ceremonies for Scrabraz. As you know, whoever is victorious this year shall gain the unparalleled accolades and esteem, to say nothing of the five million dollars prize money."

That earned a clatter of response from all around the table as silverware was smacked and glasses clinked. Sorsero was visibly delighted by the reaction, clapping along. "Excellent, I love the attitude. Let's keep that spirit going. Everyone, flip your plates over. On it, you will find the location for your first bout. Head there immediately because anyone not en route within fifteen minutes will be disqualified. The arenas are that way." Sorsero gesture behind him, where a new host of banners seemed to have sprouted up without warning, leading deeper into the island.

Before Action could mutter a single question, the stampede started. The others tore up from the table so fast that many did serious damage, leaving chunks of splinters behind. Glad he'd taken the advice of a light breakfast, Action flipped his plate over and saw a number 3. He had less than fifteen minutes to figure out what that meant, and then whatever time was remaining to determine what the hell it was he was supposed to do here.

5

Scrabraz Island was huge, even larger than it seemed upon landing. Despite hurrying and keeping a keen eye peeled, Action feared he'd be late to his first match. There was just *so much* ground to cover. On the way over, he'd passed several other numbered fields: number 5 was above a waterfall, number 1 in some sort of ice cavern, and number 7 was precariously near a sheer cliff face. Mercifully, field number 3 proved to be somewhat more normal.

Grass, a few trees nearby, and lots of dense brush around the edges. That, and the guy loaded up in weaponry, were what awaited Action as he stumbled onto the field. Overhead, he heard the whizz of tiny blades from the half-dozen drones hovering, filming the spectacle that was about to start. Action imagined the viewers were quite curious what was coming next, a sentiment he deeply echoed. Amidst all the work to actually find this place, there hadn't been any spare time to focus on what he'd actually do upon arrival.

In Action's pockets, both the visible and the hidden, were a small array of illusions and tools. The bulk of his equipment was in his trunk, which he hadn't bothered to bring to breakfast, so he was going to have to pull a performance off with just what was on-hand.

"Competitors: Introduce yourselves!" The voice of Sorsero echoed out from all the drones, and Action's opponent gave a thumbs up.

"Hardy Artillery, Munitions-style." Hardy looked over to Action, who quickly took the hint.

"Action Kadabra. Sorry, didn't know we needed a style too." Action could feel Hardy's stare intensifying; he was giving away his own inexperience. Well, in for a penny, in for a pound. "I don't suppose you'd mind explaining what we're doing?"

That earned him a loud laugh from Hardy, who reached onto his belt and pulled off a silver orb. A few quick motions and suddenly there was now a red light glowing in the orb's center. "A clueless one, huh? I've heard you pop up occasionally. Don't worry, nothing at all to fret about. We're just going to play a little game of catch. I'll toss this over, and you do your best to grab it."

That was a bit hard to believe, but maybe Hardy was taking the lead with this act? Then again, it *was* a competition, perhaps playing along with someone else's show wasn't the smartest move. Before Action could fully discern the correct strategy, Sorsero's voice came from the drones once more.

"Contestants, Round One has begun!"

Hardy didn't waste a second; the moment he'd gotten permission, he hurled the orb directly at Action, strong arms pulling off a nearly flawless throw. Action could see the orb's path, tracking it perfectly. Compared to Pop and Grandad's drills on what to do when your knife-thrower missed, the thing practically moved in slow motion. The obvious trick would be to catch it; however, Action expected if he did, there was a good chance he'd end up covered in feathers, shaving cream, or something equally ridiculous that would burst out. This was a competition. It would only make sense to leave an opponent looking silly. But letting it fall wasn't much of a show for those watching either.

Ultimately, Action decided to go through with the trick, only slightly altered. Using coordination and dexterity that most could only dream of, he caught the orb as it drew near and continued moving the object along. Keeping the pace constant, Action spun his entire body with the orb, never jostling or altering its momentum, hurling the object right back to its source. As he saw it, this was the best outcome, the trick still went off and someone else looked the fool. Perhaps not the nicest tactic, but he was only giving Hardy back his own attack.

There was just enough time for Hardy's face to realize what had happened, jerking his hands to try and recreate Action's technique. Sadly, thick as his arms were, they were laden down with too much gear. Even if he'd had the care to catch it, there simply wasn't enough speed. The orb slammed into Hardy's chest, offering Action a brief moment to wonder why he looked so downright terrified.

The explosion literally knocked Action from his feet, despite the distance. Multiple detonations rocked the grove. Evidently the rest of Hardy's gear was going up too, sending smoke and some sort of thick liquid into the air. As Action wiped some away and saw the dark red on his hands, he realized what this was: blood. Blood and... chunks, as Action noted a fleshy piece splat onto the grass nearby.

Finally daring to look up, he saw what was akin to a crater where Hardy had been standing, nothing more than a pair of smoking feet still stuffed into thick black combat boots. Looking at the absolute carnage that remained, Action was filled with a horrifying, undeniable realization.

"I totally lost this one." There was nothing he had on him, even in his repertoire, that could compete with an illusion like this one. Everything was so real. The heat, the lingering flames, the raining viscera, maybe the shoes were overkill but they did set a scene. However Hardy had pulled this off, the man must be an absolute genius of his craft, which Action speculated to be some sort of special effects.

Not long after the words left his lips, the drones issued a contradictory statement. "Look at that! We have our first victory of Round One, and it goes to Action Kadabra on field number 3. Everyone else, we suggest you step up your efforts. There can be only one champion, and someone is clearly here to strive for the title."

Very weird. Maybe because Action had sort of stolen the trick, he got credit for the success of it? That still felt like stretching, though.

A slight pause, or maybe some mumbling, then Sorsero continued. "Those whose matches conclude may head to the Hallowed Hall for rest and repair. The others will be along, except for those that won't."

Scanning the grove, Action looked to see if he could spot Hardy's cowering form, hiding from the camera to avoid spoiling the scene. "Hardy? You around here? I think we can head back together." No response other than the crackle of flames from the grass near the smoking feet. Maybe he wanted to clean up first—pulling off that kind of trick *had* to involve getting messy. In fact, Action guessed that all the supposed guns and military equipment had probably been stuffed with this fake blood and meat, which could be how Hardy made it seem so real.

From the brush, one of the identically dressed island workers stepped into view, motioning for Action to follow.

He would see Hardy later on and congratulate him on a show well performed. For the moment, Action dearly wanted a shower. All of the fake blood was soaking into his clothes and hair, and it was getting disgusting.

The only way it could have been worse is if the gore was genuine.

6

____

Upon arrival at the Hallowed Hall, Action was checked over by more silent staff clad in matching uniforms. When they found him unharmed, he was permitted to walk past the entrance, deeper into the building, where he was greeted by one of the most opulent, luxurious spreads he'd seen anywhere off the Vegas Strip. Lounging chairs and couches dotted the vast ballroom, as did all manner of food set up at various stations. There were small bars manned by staff holding cocktail shakers, as well as an area with a more varied selection of mind-altering offerings. Overlooking it all was a tremendous screen that dominated an entire massive wall.

Currently, it was projecting eight matchup brackets, two of which were already showing winners. It seemed Action and someone named Crystalbrawler on field 6 were the only ones done. As Action watched, the screen suddenly shifted as on field 7 a winner was crowned. Killossus had beaten Bernie Sensation, whoever those people were. With the other matches still going on, Action helped himself to more food, no longer quite so weighed down by a hangover or nerves.

Through the next hour, more matches were decided, and others started wandering in. He noticed that, generally speaking, whoever won their match would arrive several minutes before the losers. Curiously, not all the losers did seem to be returning, including Hardy Artillery. Perhaps some tricks needed longer to recover from, or people were actually getting injured out there? In a situation like this, with so much on the line, Action understood the desire to try risky illusions, but he didn't think the danger justified the gamble. At even the notion, he could hear his Pop and Grandad yammering on about the care a magician had to show for themselves as well as their tools.

Tim was one of the last to arrive, trailed only by the woman he'd defeated, Chef Brunoise, who was wearing a white jacket that lacked its right arm sleeve, but otherwise looked unbothered. Stang had just finished getting his first drink, so both arrived near Action at roughly the same time. It was a good thing, too, because not long after, the room's lights went dim as Sorsero's voice echoed forth.

"Our first round is completed, and what a spectacle it has already been. Yet there is still a formality that must be attended. Some of you are familiar with your competition, while others have not been properly introduced. We allow the element of surprise for the first bout; however, experience teaches that things are more fun, for the viewers, when opponents have time to strategize. So please enjoy this recap of our first round, and an introduction to your competition."

The screen flicked just as Action chomped down into a delicious shrimp. On it, he could see the guy in cowboy boots lying on the ground, grasping his stomach between bouts of vomiting blood. Standing over him was the familiar form of Steven Cage, wobbling slightly, perhaps out of fear or exhaustion, he was certainly sweating enough. "On Field 1, Steven Cage's Hollywood-style defeated Tex

Western's Cowboy-style thanks to a covert preemptive gastral strike."

Both Tim and Action looked to one another, equally confused about what that meant, until Stang leaned in and whispered, "They were one field over, and I heard Steven offer him a pre-match toast as a sing of respect. Looks like someone's glass had more than just champagne."

Before any follow-ups could be asked, the screen changed, showing a man sporting a bright floral shirt and sunglasses staring across at someone clad head-to-toe in a beekeeper's outfit wielding a long metal net that glinted sharply in the sunlight. An unheard cue was given, and both sprang into action. The beekeeper raced forward, net extended in some sort of technique for an attack. What it was didn't prove to matter, as seconds later the entire form detonated in an explosion on par with Hardy Artillery's. "While both had trouble finding their arena, once the bout kicked off, Rocket Launcher Dave's Rocket Launcher-style proved more than Bug Battler's Net-style could handle."

"Rocket Launcher Dave!" The same man from the video thrust both arms into the arm, earning light applause from the generally silent staff. Action looked around but couldn't find Bug Battler before his own face filled the screen.

Just as he'd expected, the fight between Action and Hardy on Field 3 was played in highlights as Sorsero explained what they were seeing. "Action Kadabra, using a style yet to be identified, defeated Hardy Artillery's Munitions-style with only a single move and barely any effort. Keep an eye on this one, he's wily."

Tim clapped him on the back, while Stang looked mildly distraught. "You didn't name your style? At *this* tournament? I'll say this, you have got some brass ones on you."

Gunfire filled the air, or rather, the sound of it as they watched on-screen while Don Ron unloaded into the man wearing the dirty cloak. His violin case had sprouted a trigger and was currently firing far too many rounds into a single person. It seemed that way, at least, until the cloaked man let out an ear-splitting howl. What should have been a corpse leapt from the ground, covered in fur with flashing claws and teeth. Even Sorsero sounded somewhat delighted by the sudden shift.

"Although Don Ron's Don't Worry About It-style had an excellent start on Field 4, it ultimately proved no match for Chaney Nadawuf's Primal-style. Took our staff quite a bit of healing to patch up Don Ron, at that."

A clatter of a plate sounded from nearby, as a far more shaken Don Ron nearly dropped his platter of crab legs. The once pristine suit had been ripped to shreds, yet the man himself appeared remarkably unharmed. Action still wasn't entirely sure how this contest worked, but he was hoping to catch-on before the next bout.

"On Field 5, we had a battle of the blade between Tim Burly's Lumberjack-style and Chef Brunoise's Culinary-style." Suddenly, the screen was full of movement. Tim was up there, dashing and diving far faster than his build would imply. But Chef Brunoise was no slouch either, slinging and swinging a seemingly endless supply of knives. Tim deflected most of the ranged shots, only allowing a few shallow cuts into his legs, while steadily advancing. Occasionally, he'd hurl a throwing axe to buy breathing room, all in the efforts of making the fight melee.

At last he reached her, and the pair were a blur of swinging limbs. Chef Brunoise had produced a pair of cleavers that were nearly able to keep pace with Tim, but "nearly" wasn't good enough. With a set of well-timed strikes, Tim knocked both cleavers away then swept upward with his axe, taking Chef Brunoise's entire right arm off in the process.

"Still got a little on me from that," Tim muttered, pointing to the streak of red barely visible on his plaid shirt. Action realized he was still coated in the faux viscera from his own bout. No one had offered him a chance to clean-up yet, much as he'd have loved the opportunity. "Good thing the staff can regrow limbs. I'll want a rematch with her one day."

"Yeah right," Action chuckled. "That would be amazing."

"Oh, they do it alright," Stang confirmed. "How do you think she has a new one? Or Don Ron isn't half-chewed? Scrabraz has all sorts of magic; its why they hold the tournament here. Anything less than real death can be repaired."

Tim's hand splatted down on Action's shoulder, knocking a few stuck-on bits to the ground. "Good news is, that means your gun-happy buddy won't be coming for payback. Not even Scrabraz can put all this back together." For emphasis, Tim rubbed his dripping fingers together, sending splotches to the ground.

All at once, the truth hit Action, just about the time he realized going so hard on the shrimp might have been a bad idea. Grabbing the nearest container he could find, Action buried his head inside and let everything come rushing out.

7

It was crazy, even the notion that this was real. Who would gather a bunch of strangers together on a weird island and have them fight, potentially to the death? Even as Action formed the question, his mind flashed to the countless high-rollers he'd encountered through the years, ones with more money than drive, and the general way they regarded human life that wasn't theirs. Okay, so it was entirely possible a person would put this together, but why would everyone else show up? They couldn't all have made the same mix-up. Was it just for the money, or was there more at work?

By the time Action pulled himself together enough to lift his head from the potted plant he'd filled with half-digested shrimp, the screen was showing a defeated River Slayer slump over unconscious, the giant padded figure who'd stopped bullets evidently proving too much to handle. Action had missed the play-by-play in all the digestive antics and was working incredibly hard to convince himself that it was merely colored syrup and hamburger meat covering him. Blatant denial was his only hope of not having a full-on freak out before he could get to a shower.

"Can't go so hard on the seafood; that's a rookie move." Tim offered Action a sip of something dark and alcoholic, which he accepted. The burn of the booze helped wash away the lingering singe of stomach acid, not to mention momentarily soothing his nerves.

Overhead, the screen flickered, showing a familiar face set against a pair of opponents. Stang was staring down a woman in overalls holding a gigantic gator on a chain leash. Sorsero's voice arrived soon to add commentary. "On Field 7, Stang used his Jelly-style against Leatherlegs and Earl's Swamp-style. In the end, it turned out two heads were not better than one."

The Stang on screen shot forward, like he was trying to get chomped. Earl the gator took a mighty bite, Stang slipping away at the last moment. Leatherlegs was no slouch, swinging a machete for Stang's head, but the moment he landed a strike to her arm, the weapon went clattering to the ground. Another few short strikes, and Leatherlegs dropped alongside her machete. Earl kept on coming, but luckily Stang was faster. Although his attacks weren't as effective against the reptile, eventually he was able to wear the beast down.

"How are you doing that? Some sort of ancient nerve disruption technique?" Tim peered across the table to the his fast-made friend, looking him over like it was for the first time.

Stang shook his head, pairing it with a well-time eyeroll and a sip of his White Russian. "That's ridiculous. I'm not sure such a tactic even exists. I was experimented on by scientists who spliced in jellyfish DNA and exposed to me some mutagenic rays, granting me a facsimile of their natural capabilities, including their painful sting." He chuckled into his drink, pausing only long enough for a wipe of his damp forehead. "Secret nerve techniques, really, somebody is reading too much battle-fiction."

A tremendous thud shook the room, interrupting their conversation along with most others in the room. Someone new had arrived, and what a someone it was. This person… animal…thing…whatever, stood ten feet tall at the apex of its head, which sat atop a long neck and ended in a pair of jaws that would give Earl the gator envy. Mottled gray skin ran the length of its muscular body, which included two tremendous arms, several feet of tail, and legs ending in wide, flat feet. Beady yellow eyes took in the room before it sauntered forward once more, heading to one of the buffet tables.

"Just in time for his own fight footage, on Field 8 we had Killossus test his new Decimation-style against Bernie Sensation's Combustion-style, to very one-sided results."

The monster, Killossus, appeared on screen now, set against the guy who'd been wearing flames since Action first saw him. Bernie's arms and the attached nozzles on his sleeves shot up, aiming for Killossus's head. Twin bursts of flame shot forth, nearly singing the creature as it twisted out of range at the last moment. Shooting forward off a single leap, Killossus landed hard atop Bernie Sensation, slamming him onto the stone ground of their field. Clangs of metal echoed forth, and suddenly Bernie was scrambling to contend with his own outfit. Killossus stepped away, staring in what almost seemed like confusion, as Bernie ran in a circle like a dog hunting its tail, trying to fix or tweak some unseen setting that had been damaged in the attack.

When Bernie detonated moments later, it felt all-too-familiar to Action, even if this explosion was a lot more flame-based than the shower of gore Hardy's death had conjured. If he'd had more in his stomach, it would have left;

instead, he merely made sure the plant was still nearby. Never hurt to be safe.

"That catches everyone up on today's bouts," Sorsero's voice explained. "You've got several hours until the next match, so feel free to rest, train, or explore the island to your heart's content. Just be ready for your next opponent." The screen changed one last time, displaying a series of brackets. All of the original sixteen names were present; however, only eight of them moved forward. Some, like Bernie and Hardy, were crossed out entirely, a fact Action dearly wished he hadn't noticed.

As the names moved, new brackets revealed themselves, showing who would have the next matches. Tim let out a short whistle, then looked over to the cloaked man who'd shown his animal side, Chaney Nadawuf, his next opponent. As for Action, he would be going against Steven Cage. Looking across the room, he spotted the greasy-haired man, already staring right back at Action. That was probably someone to watch out for, at least when open food or drink was around.

"By the might of mesoglea, I wanted to test myself, didn't think I'd get a chance like this so soon." Stang rubbed his hands together, sending flecks of moisture raining upon the table. Action and Tim followed his eyes back to the board where they had very different reactions. Tim clapped Stang on the back, while Action paled in terror.

The next person Stang was set to fight was none other than the fearsome Killossus, who at that moment was chewing through a roast chicken, bones and all.

8

Between various syrups, glitters, flame-retarding gels, and other skin adhesives, Action Kadabra was a man well-versed in scrubbing his body hard. Standing in his expansive, luxurious shower, he scoured his arms, even though the last of the blood had long since faded down the drain. It was a body much too muscular for classic magic, honed specifically for Action's particular stage persona. His Pop and Grandad hated it, both the moniker and the act, not that Action had expected any less. Their unwillingness to evolve or take new chances was what had driven him out of the family act in the first place. Then again, neither of them had ended up covered in gore on some sort of murder island, so maybe they'd had some wisdom after all. At least he was staying somewhere nice.

Once the results of Round One had been fully announced, they were led to their rooms in the Hallowed Hall by the silent staff. So far as Action could tell, each was the same: huge luxurious suites with four-poster beds, high-end furniture, and TVs bigger than the window in Action's studio apartment.

The opulence was somewhat marred by the bloody foot-prints leading to the shower, but there was no other way for Action to get clean. Besides, at that point, concern for a housekeeping bill was the lowest issue on his mind. He was a lot more pre-occupied with the idea that he was in some sort fighting tournament where death was very much on the line. Now that the remains were off of him, Action had found a sense of peace with what happened to Hardy. Someone had tried to kill Action, and without knowing the context, Action had defended himself. Even if he'd been fully aware, there was mental refuge in the fact that he hadn't attacked, only reflected what was sent his way.

That didn't mean he wasn't going to need a lot of booze and therapy to get the image of a man exploding from his mind, but it did allow him to focus on the more pressing matters at hand, such as the fact that he had another match coming later in the day. At least his was only against Steven Cage. Outside of masked henchmen and poison, he didn't seem too dangerous. Action shook his head, letting a spray of hot water blast away the complacency. That was exactly the sort of thinking that had likely gotten Tex Western a belly full of poison. Although, if he could lose one of these bouts safely, that might be the easiest way out.

Shutting off the shower, Action flew through toweling off, then dove into his luggage for a fresh outfit. Tank-top, high-waisted synthetic fiber pants containing countless hidden pockets, and thick specialty boots with extra support built in for low-arches. Pausing to throw some gel in his hair and make sure he had a few tools stowed away, Action dashed out into the hallway, a new plan solidifying in his mind.

He would lose. That was the easiest, safest way out of all this. Yes, not winning five million dollars would blow, but seeing people turned into mush made working Off-Strip seem not so bad in comparison. Losing was better, and luckily, his next opponent didn't seem to be the sort who would care about how they won. If he agreed to let Steven Cage take the victory, Action could head to the sidelines with the other losers. The ones who were still alive, anyway.

For as outstanding as the idea seemed, there was a sizable logistical issue: Action couldn't find Steven Cage anywhere. The corridors of the Hallowed Hall were sparse. It seemed most of the others were all preparing for the next bout in their own ways. Aside from the silent, uniformly dressed staff, the only people Action could find were Leatherlegs and Earl, who were still working their way through the buffet, and Stang, who was folded into some sort of yoga pose and breathing deeply. Not even Tim was around, and Action double-checked the bar to be certain.

Without warning, Action found himself stumbling onto a terrace that looked out toward the ocean. The view was astounding, a sudden panorama of paradise appearing without warning. He skidded to a stop, pausing to appreciate the beauty on what might turn out to be his last day of life. Movement in the corner of his vision stole some, though not all, of his attention.

Rising from a pair of thick stone benches were two sizable figures. Killossus turned away from the heavily padded man, who reached out to grab his shoulder but was easily shaken off. Padded man stared as Killossus walked off, shaking the hood of his coat slowly before turning and noticing Action was there.

"Sorry to interrupt," Action said hurriedly. He'd talked his way around enough drunks in bars to know these slights were best handled immediately, before egos had time to bruise.

"It's fine. Seems we were already done talking anyway." The voice was oddly composed, nearly harmonic, but also unexpectedly peaceful. While it was hard to see much more than a pair of shaded eyes through the narrow opening in the layers of cloth, they appeared to take him in. "You're Action Kadabra, the only one who beat my time in Round One."

Action nodded, unsure what the appropriate protocol was for that sort of accusation/compliment. "I have a hunch that record won't hold up through Round Two. Sorry, haven't caught your name yet."

There was a pause, unmistakable as the man looked down at his extensive coverings. "Crystalbrawler. That's what I go by…these days."

After a moment of thought, Action recalled that name from the results boards earlier. He also remembered *who* Crystalbrawler had been up against. "You beat River Slayer in almost record time? I saw her cut entirely through several people and a car with a single swing."

Crystalbrawler's shrug was barely discernable through the multiple layers. "She had an unfortunate match-up. I'm made of stouter stuff. It was her bad luck to draw the tournament's eventual winner in the first round. But then, luck is as much a part of fights as kicks, counters, or elemental-infused ranged attacks. Something to keep in mind, considering your next opponent."

"I actually think I've got something of a plan for that one," Action admitted. Calling coordinating to lose a plan was something of a stretch, but it certainly counted as a strategy.

"Be careful with him," Crystalbrawler cautioned. "Most of us are here to test ourselves and our skills against peers on our level or seek the reward, but some of us have personal reasons as well. Steven Cage has never truly recovered since the viral video of him passing out and pooping himself during a stunt. He's not just here to win—he seeks to utterly squash and humiliate his opponents, some misguided attempt to reclaim his pride, confidence, or other nonsense."

As Action thought back on the events of the weekend, he realized that if all of this was real, that meant Steven Cage had in fact brought a mercenary army to the docks in an effort to kill off some of his competition. Setting aside how outright batshit insane such a tactic was, it also spoke to a man with zero regard for life other than his own. Someone Action might not necessarily be wise to trust too much, even if he did want to hand over a victory.

"You're saying he's going to come in with backup plans?"

"I am telling you that the truly desperate are never to be underestimated." Crystalbrawler started for the terrace's exit, pausing briefly as he passed by Action. "Advice you should also keep in mind if you and I end up facing one another."

9

After his conversation with Crystalbrawler, Action continued hunting for Steven Cage, only to come up empty. It wasn't until he was heading out to the fight that he started seeing a few familiar faces leaving their rooms, and one come puffing in from what appeared to be an outdoor jog. Action waved to Tim, who gave a nod back before hurrying past, obviously in a hurry for his own match.

Finding Field 6 was easier than his last excursion, largely because Action used his downtime to peruse a map of the island. Well, "sketch" would be more appropriate, given how little detail was on the depiction, but there were large markers denoting the location of each field. Briefly, Action considered bringing his trunk along, in case he needed a few more tools than what could be concealed on those voluminous pants. That might send the wrong message, however. If he was hoping for peaceful resolution, showing up appearing armed to the teeth wasn't going to help the sell. Action *did* still stuff a few extra utilities into his hidden pants pockets, Crystalbrawler's warning still fresh in his ear.

Padding down to the shoreline, Action soon spotted huge

hanging banners denoting a battlefield. These were set up along the sand of the beach, a familiar figure already waiting as Action approached. Steven Cage stared down his opponent with no expression; evidently he'd learned enough acting to at least hide his feelings, if not project believable false ones.

"Good evening," Action called. Behind them, the sun was sinking low on the ocean's horizon, the first day of this madness nearly at its end.

"Yes, it is," Steven agreed.

Slowly, Action made his way to the beach, ignoring the buzz of overhead drones monitoring their progress. "This is all kind of crazy, right?"

"Truly insane," Steven agreed. "So much monitoring, like they don't trust us to play by the rules."

"There are rules?" After the fights and weapons Action had seen, he was genuinely shocked to hear such a notion.

Steven intently watched Action's movements as he set foot on the sand, despite the fight not being on yet. "Ridiculous, right? We're not allowed to fight outside of matches, throw a bout, attack after someone is officially defeated, so many hamstrings. This is a tournament of survival; any and all tactics should be permissible."

Action swallowed hard, sending his notion of feigning easy defeat into his stomach acid along with the spittle. If people were getting limbs lopped off while playing by the rules, he wasn't sure he could envision the punishment for breaking one. Besides, the more he talked to Steven Cage, the wiser Crystalbrawler's insight sounded. This was not a man seemingly inclined to reason.

"Hang on, if you can't attack outside of matches, what about those goons who blocked the boat?"

"We weren't on the island yet, and besides, they weren't participants. It's not my fault if a contracted strike force happened to try thinning out the fodder." Steven's hand touched the side pocket of his silk robe, fingers glancing against it like there was heat radiating off.

Overhead, the buzz rose in volume as a drone moved closer, their only warning before Sorsero's voice burst forth. "Combatants, everyone is in position. Begin Round Two!"

The instant he could, Action moved. Instinct, more than reason. He was a showman, a magician, a master of fundamental tactics like misdirection and pushes, so he could certainly recognize them in use. Steven's several-hour absence pre-fight suggested he'd been somewhere, and this was the perfect terrain to hide ground-based traps beneath. Add in the way he started talking only when Action reached a certain spot, the sand on his fingernails, and that quick touch of his pocket; all of it hinted that there was more at work than the eyes might suggest.

By the time Action was clear, Steven had yanked a remote out of his robe pocket and slammed down a button. Beneath the section where Action would have been standing, a tremendous plume burst forth, sending sand spraying across the battlefield. No doubt about it, Steven had planted traps. Bombs, by the looks of things.

Part of Action wanted to scream at the drone that this couldn't be allowed, except was it any worse than rocket launchers or giant gators? Hell, Steven even gave him a breakdown of the rules pre-fight, and preparing the grounds wasn't on that list. And *of course* he'd gone way overboard with the size of the explosions. Had they been small enough, Action might have considered a small, healable injury as an easy out, but that kind of force could turn him into...well, Hardy Artillery.

There was no time to reflect on the insanity of any of this, it was like a balancing act from childhood, trying to walk the thin rope strung between Grandad's trees. Start focusing on the ground, that's where you'd end up. Action's only choice was to stay upright until he found the safety of solid footing once more. In this case, that meant not dying before escaping back to the mainland. Action dashed along the sand, light steps allowing him to race along the top without sinking too far in. That proved frustrating to Steven, whose clicks on the remote were always a hair behind, showering Action in sand as he dodged and weaved, never staying on a predictable path. It was a daring race of who would falter first; one that soon had a front-runner as Action closed the gap between them.

Just as Action arrived, fist half-cocked, Steven put up his arms in surrender, even going so far as to drop the remote. "Okay, okay. Looks like you got me. I obviously can't set off a bomb this close to both of us. I had my tactics; you were just faster." Slowly lowering his arms, Steven extended a hand. "You fought well and should be proud."

With barely more than a glance, Action accepted the shake, gripping Steven's wrist using both hands. The sudden twist of glee in the actor's sweaty face appeared without warning as he made a quick motion with the currently shaking hand. That same smile quickly faded as Action continued starting right back, sporting a grin of his own, only Action's came with a short side of commentary.

"Here's the thing about retractable wrist blades: they use the same spring and mount mechanisms as a lot of other tools, especially those in the world of illusion. Yours has a latch that's very easy to pop, assuming someone knows what to do and has excellent sleight of hand skills."

A sharp *twang* sang through the air, causing Steven to look down in shock at the blade that had been stolen from his own wrist in the span of seconds and turned back around to pierce its owner. Moments after he realized the blade broke the skin, Steven stumbled back, already shaking as his hands went to his stomach.

"Guessing that was poisoned, so if you used anything too strong, now is a good time to quit and call for medical attention." Action might not want to die, but that wasn't the same as being okay with murder. Well, intentional murder, anyway.

"I am not going to lose." Steven stopped his backtrack, finding an unexpected stretch of resolve. He took a shuddering step forward. "I want my fame back, and it starts at this tournament. I am not going to lose. I am not..." He trailed off, the sweat on his forehead increasing exponentially. "I am not going to...not going too... Oh god, not again!"

Crumpling to the ground, Steven clutched his stomach as a new series of sounds tore forth, these far less verbal or composed. As he curled into a ball, a flood of rear-waste absolutely ruining his current pants, the drones buzzed softly overhead.

"On Field 6, Action Kadabra has officially defeated Steven Cage."

Standing on the sand, Action suddenly found himself at a crossroads. With Hardy, there hadn't been fallout to manage besides the shower, but Steven Cage was still alive. Alive, and in a lot of pain. Granted, he'd been trying to use the same poison on Action, so pity was limited, but the smell was starting to become an issue.

Turning to head back, Action found himself staring down a half-dozen of the island's silent workers, several holding large objects. As two loaded Steven onto a stretcher and dragged him away, the others setup a small but hefty table, laptop, tray of fruits and cheeses, and a bottle of champagne complete with an ice-filled chilling bucket. One of the workers poured Action a glass while another led him to a comfortable chair next to the table. The laptop's screen suddenly flashed, showing footage of another battle.

"Congratulations to Action Kadabra and Crystalbrawler, who have both already completed their matches and are enjoying the spoils of victory. While we're cutting together your highlight reels, feel free to enjoy the live entertainment still in progress."

Without warning, the screen flashed away to Tim, slamming an axe into Chaney Nadawuf's belly and carving it around, a move that should have spilled the man's guts onto the slick surface of the ice cavern they were battling in. Instead, the wound healed nearly as fast as it was formed, refusing intestines the chance to become out-testines. Snarling, Chaney whipped a furry, clawed hand for Tim's torso, only to snare a few threads of plaid fiber when he suddenly ducked away.

"That all you got? The netherwolves who try to steal our town tree's sacred sap are far more ferocious, going to have to be better."

Snapping and ripping filled the air as Chaney seemed to agree with the assessment. He grew at a shocking rate, mass almost doubling in mere seconds as the dirty cloak finally ripped away to nothing. Towering over Tim, Chaney's muzzle let out a rough snort, somehow appearing excited by the development.

"Yope. That might about do it."

The screen suddenly changed, loading a new image before Action's eyes. Stang was running around a graveyard, quite a morose field option to draw, while Killossus followed in tight pursuit. They were using highly different tactics, Stang relying on dexterity to dodge about the stone headstones, zigzagging to capitalize on his greater mobility. Killossus, on the other hand, had elected brute force as his tactic. In fairness, it was working quite well as the giant beast smashed through headstone after headstone, never letting Stang widen the gap by too much.

"Get back here!" Killossus paused briefly, rubbing his left eye, and Action noticed the swelling around it. So Stang had managed to score a hit, and what stinging ability he had was strong enough to affect Killossus. It didn't seem like the move had gone over well, given the way Killossus was tearing after him.

Action swallowed hard, images of Hardy's remains rising up once more. He'd known Stang and Tim for all of a day, but they were also the only friends he had in this ludicrous situation. Besides which, a day was more than long enough not to want to see someone bitten in half by a semi-human creature. Leaning forward in his seat, Action gulped as Killossus suddenly leapt, crossing a huge amount of the distance, and landing worryingly close to Stang. Moving fast, Stang dove behind a headstone just before Killossus's tail knocked the thing in half. By the time the rubble landed, Stang was already gone, shooting across the graveyard in a dead sprint.

Another flash of the screen and they were back to Tim and Chaney. Already, the cavern looked different: huge slash marks could be seen along several of the ice-covered walls, the same size as the claws that swung for Tim's spine as he rolled across the ground. There was a muffled thud as Tim smacked against his own bag of axes; evidently they'd come off sometime during the fight.

The momentary delay was all Chaney needed, leaping on top of Tim just like he had Don Ron, except last time Chaney hadn't been nearly as large or furry. Action's heart sank right along with those slobbering jaws as they inched closer to Tim's face. After a chewing from that beast, there might not be enough left to heal.

A new flash, this time not a changing of the screen. No, it was movement, the glimmer of a strike delivered so fast and precise, the camera couldn't even capture it properly. For a moment, the pair stayed there, the werewolf standing over his prize. Then, softly, Chaney's head dipped forward, falling away from the neck entirely. As it tumbled, his body began to shudder and warp, shifting back to human form while Tim climbed back to his feet.

In his hands was a gleaming axe, silver along the head and roughly half of the handle. "Almost didn't find that fountain before our match, but it looks like the axes of my ancestors were with me today."

"On Field 1, Tim Burly has officially defeated Chaney Nadawuf." Sorsero's voice gave Action a start. By the time he recovered, the feed was back to Stang's fight. Within seconds, Action wished it hadn't changed. While Tim had pulled off a surprise win against Chaney, things weren't shaping up nearly so well for Stang.

He was crawling now, blood down his back along with claw marks, and Action spotted a few headstones that looked like they'd been ripped up and thrown. If any of those had clipped Stang, it would certainly explain why his legs were out of use. Killossus, meanwhile, was slowly stalking up on his prey. The fight was over, it had to be, so why wasn't Stang giving up?

"Yield." Killossus was only a few feet away now, voice more hiss than human, yet the words were still discernable. "Now."

Silently, Action urged Stang to take the out, even as his friend's head shook. Weakly, he raised a single arm and extended a middle finger. "Come and make me."

There were no second chances with Killossus. With alarming speed, he dashed forward, jaws already opened wide. Action looked away at the last moment, but he still heard the *crunch*. Inch-by-inch, he forced his eyes open, revealing both what he had expected, and hadn't. Stang grimaced in pain, gripping the stump where his arm used to be, but there was also a dash of triumph in that expression.

Killossus, on the other hand, was running around, smacking his tongue and mouth in vain. Most of Stang's arm lay on the grass nearby, minus chunks of the hand, covered in drool and a few bite marks. As Killossus scrambled about, Stang tilted his head back, laughing through the agony.

"*Now*, I yield. Had to make you earn it."

Killossus looked for a moment like he might chew right through Stang in fury, except he was too occupied by the discomfort in his mouth. Moments later, the island's workers came strolling into view, followed shortly by Sorsero's voice.

"On Field 4, Killossus has defeated Stang. That ends our fights for today. Tomorrow we begin the final rounds. Rest up, everyone. Our final four contenders are sure to put on an outstanding show."

In all the excitement, Action had nearly forgotten about the other implications. Grabbing the champagne glass, he hammered down the contents in a single gulp. There was a one-in-three chance he'd be up against Killossus tomorrow.

Which meant he only had one night to find a way to survive.

Once the match was done, Action was led back to the Hallowed Hall by the unsettlingly silent workers. Upon entering, he took one look and nearly blanched. The room's entire layout had been reshuffled. Now several larger tables were lined up next to one another, while a far more extravagant seating arrangement was waiting with four place settings. If that weren't obvious enough, one of the chairs was over-sized and made of steel, clearly intended for a larger-than-human competitor.

The stares of his fellow beaten competitors felt greasy against Action's skin as he made his way toward the table. He was so tense that when a hand suddenly clapped down on his shoulder, it took the entirety of his stage-training not to let out a terrified yelp. Not that it would have mattered, no one was beating Tim in the decibel department.

"Bout time you made it back!" Several more good-hearted slaps made it clear Tim was in high spirits. "Great fight, just watched the highlights. You were amazing, looking like a helpless lamb until it was time to strike."

"Thanks," Action mumbled, before managing to find a

more optimistic tone. "Caught the end of yours, it was incredible. So you went and turned an axe into silver before the fight?"

Tim nodded, a sudden shadow of pain twinkling in those eyes, one of the few visible parts of the massive bearded face. "Was a real shame to do that to Ol' Betsy, she's not fit to bite the bark ever again, but a tool serves the purpose. Today, I needed a silver axe, and her sacrifice made this possible. Otherwise, I'd have been lucky to end up like Stang."

At the mention of the missing tournament member, Action's head whipped around, searching the room. If Don Ron had been healable after his bout, there was no reason a missing arm should be the end of Stang, yet Action's gut still twisted as he hunted around the empty room.

"He's at the bar," Tim supplied helpfully.

Sure enough, there was Stang, walking over with a White Russian in what had to be the largest glass that the bar stocked. As he approached, Action noticed something was different. The arm that had been chomped off was indeed restored, except it didn't quite match the rest of Stang. Seeing the comparison, it was obvious his current skin color was slightly more purple, not to mention slimier. Stang gave the arm a waggle, like he was trying to wake it up.

"How you feeling? Everything okay?" Even seeing the restored limb before him, Action couldn't believe that in such a short time such brutal wounds had been healed.

"More or less," Stang said, shaking his arm once more. "The healing regenerated my arm, but it came out as the base model. Have to wait for the jellyfish DNA to seep over and re-mutate it. Going to be a few days before I'm back at full strength, plus the damn thing is all pins and needles." Punctuating his words with a hefty drink, this cream-based cocktail was clearly intended for more than social sipping.

With a solemn nod, Tim gently patted Stang's head. "You

fought well. Killossus is a strong opponent. At this point, every combatant is highly dangerous. Even Rocket Launcher Dave lost his bout with Crystalbrawler."

"Guess he dodged?" Action was joking, but there was little funny about the excited gleam in Tim's eyes.

"Nope."

Loud steps pulled everyone's attention to the front of the hall, and Action spun around expecting to see Killossus. Instead, what awaited him appeared to be a stranger, and one who certainly lived up to the title. While a few patches of skin were visible, largely around the face, most of this man was covered in crystalline rocks, winding around his torso, built up thick around his fists and feet, mounds poking out from his back and shoulders. If not for the few scraps of singed fabric, Action might not have realized this was formerly the contender covered entirely in thick padded clothing.

Crystalbrawler paid no mind to the stares of the room as he steadily walked forward, eyes only on the next step ahead. Without the dense wrappings around his feet, every step echoed across the stone floor. Just when Action felt like he might suffocate from the tension in the room, Sorsero's voice boomed forth, a welcome interruption for once.

"Welcome, everyone, to the end of our tournament's first day! While our guests find their seats, enjoy a highlight reel from today's events."

"Guess that's my cue to join the other losers." Stang slapped Tim on the shoulder, returning his favorite gesture. "Go put those axes to work. As for you, Action, you're just full of surprises. Keep it up, because it only gets harder from here."

Those were words Action really didn't need to hear as he numbly moved toward the elaborate table. Overhead, a gigantic projector screen was showing scenes from their battles thus far. As Action turned there was a replay of his own victory over Steven Cage, who was curiously absent from the dinner. That thought might have gotten more attention if the screen hadn't flipped over in that moment, showing a still fully clothed Crystalbrawler and Rocket Launcher Dave.

What happened next, Action might not have believed if not for the day he'd already had. Rocket Launcher Dave was showing exceptional dexterity, running for the trees lining Field 3. He was quick and nimble, proving there was more to his style than lining up a shot, and his activity was contrasted all the more by Crystalbrawler who stood there. Waiting.

When the shot finally came, Action was still expecting the covered figure to dodge, no matter what evidence suggested had actually happened. He just couldn't fathom someone taking a hit like that, not until he saw it happen. Explosion, flames, and then suddenly, movement. Crystalbrawler tore out of the burning foliage, his clothing already ablaze, bearing down on Rocket Launcher Dave like a locomotive with a grudge. One punch from those crystal-covered fists was all it took. Rocket Launcher Dave dropped to the ground, bright red rivers of blood already surging from his nose.

Meaning not only was Crystalbrawler incredibly strong, he'd now shrugged off bullets and an explosion before Action's eyes. Between him and Killossus, the next round was looking more and more dangerous. Setting his resolve, Action decided it was time to stop playing things so passively. He wasn't just going to sit back and accept his fate of being brutally beaten and potentially beheaded. It was time for him to use his skills and take things into his own hands.

Tonight, once everyone was asleep, Action would try to escape.

When Action was a child, long before he'd chosen his own moniker, sneaking was a daily part of life. Pop and Granddad were adamant that the ability to go unseen was one of a magician's most fundamental utilities. Whether it was disappearing on stage, skulking through the audience, or obfuscating a single limb for the sake of a trick; controlling what others saw was a foundation in the art of illusion, one that they'd been determined Action would hone.

If he was spotted crawling his way to dinner, that meant half-dessert. Caught slinking to the bathroom, that was an extra half-hour of drilling card tricks. And heaven help Action if he lost a game of Hide-and-Seek in the first hour. Growing up, there were other magicians who would suddenly arrive at their dated manor, begging Pop and Grandpa to "put them through the program." Most lasted less than a day, some endured it for over a week, but occasionally, they would take an aspiring magician into that basement only for a rising superstar to emerge years later. Once it was finally Action's turn to mosey down those concrete steps, he only wished the option of quitting was available. Not for him, though. He had the Kadabra legacy to carry on.

Despite all the trouble their training had caused him growing up, Action couldn't help being thankful to his teachers as he silently padded along the stone floor, narrowly ducking into an alcove just as some of the silent workers crossed through his stretch of hallway. Getting out of the room was easy enough, and he'd been making steady progress creeping his way to freedom. Past that, Action didn't have much of a plan to go on. There had to be more ships bringing in supplies. Fresh food was constantly being set-out and he'd yet to see a single farm or even worker hauling a wheelbarrow. If he could reach one of those ships, Action felt confident he could effectively disappear, even if someone came looking. It was one of the tricks he'd always been particularly adept at.

Slinking across the stones, Action paused regularly, waiting to be sure no other workers might catch his escape attempt. Nearly there, just a short stairway down and a few more halls to the nearest exit. As he was edging his foot forward, a voice rang out, nearly causing him to leap as it shattered the silence Action had been cloaked in.

"I wouldn't recommend running."

Action turned, so quiet even his blood pumped softly, to find Crystalbrawler sitting in a large chair, sizable metal mug gripped in his right hand, barely visible through all the rocks encasing the limb. There was no aggression in his expression, or as much as one could read through the mineral covering, as he motioned to the open chairs nearby. This area must be some sort of lounge. Behind them, the wind whipped through the trees on the shoreline, stirring up dark waves on the seemingly endless ocean.

"There are rules to this place. You think it's scary now, wait until you see someone step out of line." A long, languished slurp from the metal mug punctuated his advice. "But I'm not going to blow the whistle on you. Try to escape if you want, whether you succeed or fail, one less person to get through on the way to Killossus."

A wary look shot from his eye to the mug, as if he blamed it for the looseness of his own lips. Deciding that he should probably know more about what punishment was in store on an island with magical healing and blasé attitudes toward killing, Action switched courses, stepping into the lounge with Crystalbrawler. While an open bar beckoned, Action made no move for refreshments. The escape might still be on, and he'd want all his wits about him.

"Can you tell me more?" Seeing as Crystalbrawler had said there were rules to more than just combat, as in plural, better to learn about the full parameters of this place before accidentally breaking one.

"Eh, why not." With a resolute chug, Crystalbrawler drained the remains of the metal mug, then hefted himself out of the chair to begin fixing another. "We were both here last year. Been rivals since we first fought, and we both get the tap for the same tournament. Felt like fate, you know? Setting us up for a big final showdown, one last match to determine the best."

It was fairly clear by this point that Crystalbrawler had interpreted "can you tell me more" as applying to a very different subject. Action wracked his brain for a way to steer things back on track, but now that he was going, Crystalbrawler let the story burst forth, unable to hold it back any longer.

"Except we both lost in Round Two. Got our asses stomped, matter of fact. It was just like this one, people with weapons, special abilities, one guy kept forming and throwing balls of energy. No place for a normal martial artist, no way for us to defeat their inhuman power. So when a representative from a genetic research company approached us at the end, offering access to power we'd never seen, Killaby couldn't resist."

There was a lot to take in during that half-sloshed tirade, not the least of which was Killossus's real name being Killaby, but Action couldn't help noticing one glaring omission in the tale. "Guess they offered you something a little more...earthy."

Looking down at himself, almost like he was surprised, Crystalbrawler lifted his newly filled mug in a mock toast. "Found this on my own. Had to seek out the Songlehelm Crystal Caverns and defeat The Shattered Guardian, but I was permitted to drink from the Well of the Creation Stone. After I heard what they'd done to Killaby, I knew I had to be strong enough."

"To defeat him?"

There was an unmistakable sadness in the shake of Crystalbrawler's head, even as stiff as it was. "To end his suffering. Look at what they've done to him, he seems barely even capable of more than grunting a few words anymore. We might have been rivals, but that came with a certain amount of respect. I can't let him go on that way; I have to set what's still human inside free." Closing his right hand into a fist, suddenly a sharp hunk of crystal shot forth, extending a full three feet into a roughly formed blade.

"I have to do more damage than even this island can heal. I have to cut off Killossus's head, tear out his heart, and burn whatever remains. It's the only way to save him."

With a deep gulp, Action decided that perhaps he'd learned all he really needed to. Backing up, he was shocked at the sensation of a body blocking his path, especially considering he hadn't heard so much as a sigh or soft step while they'd been talking.

"What a fun little get-together. I hope you don't mind if I join in as well." Sorsero stepped out from behind Action, moving without creating so much as a whisper.

It seemed Action wasn't the only one on the island talented at sneaking around.

13

____

From the bar, Sorsero produced a bottle of vibrant green liquid, pouring himself a healthy glass filled nearly to the brim before ambling back over to join Action and Crystalbrawler. "A little something to keep me spry. Help yourself, if you aren't afraid of side effects." A long swig from the glass, and Sorsero briefly had a green liquid mustache before licking it away.

"Now then, how is everyone enjoying the tournament so far? We're always looking for ways to improve."

"The buffet could use more veggie options," Crystalbrawler replied. Action held his breath, half-waiting for a battalion of the silent workers to materialize and slice off Crystalbrawler's lips for speaking out of turn.

Instead, Sorsero let out a few clucks under his breath. "It's a balancing act, budget-wise. Most competitors are all about the protein, and what goes uneaten there can easily be re-used. Vegetables rot much faster, and demand tends to be limited at these events. Still, every time one of you asks for better options, it gives me more ammunition to change things, so I appreciate the feedback."

Eye still scanning about for an approaching assassination squad, Action let out a slow breath of relief as it became clear things weren't about to take a homicidal turn. Well, if Sorsero was in such a good mood, might as well try and get some help of his own.

"My chief complaint would be lack of clarity on the rules," Action admitted. "Some people have weapons; some have special powers. We aren't allowed to fight outside of matches, except when one of us is dispatching a hit squad on half the others. Oh, and apparently rigging a battlefield with bombs is no big deal?" By the end, Action was starting to get worked up, his bottled-up feelings at the madness of the situation attempting to fully burst forth.

"Ah yes, Mr. Cage." Sorsero slurped more of the green juice, unconcerned with any discomfort his sounds might be causing. "He does love to skirt the edge of our rules, but if he's adept at one thing, it's on staying *just* inside the lines. The boat attack, for example, occurred before you'd set foot on the vessel, which is island property. Until you boarded, the rules were not in effect."

Crystalbrawler was nodding along like this made perfect sense, so Action bit back an objection about what a ridiculous distinction it seemed. That was for the best anyway, as Sorsero wasn't finished answering yet. "As for the bombs on the beach...you had the same amount of warning as he did, I believe. Had you raced off to prepare the field ahead of time, you'd have seen him at work and gained forewarning of his plans. Preparation is as much a part of battle as blades and fists."

This point, Action had a harder time rebutting. As a magician, much of his art was predicated upon preparation: setting up gimmicks, readying the stage, sometimes even peppering plants through an audience. He wasn't entirely sure the principle should apply to a deadly fighting tournament but had no room to throw stones regardless.

"At any rate," Sorsero continued, "I wouldn't worry too much about the rules. By this point, I imagine you've gleaned any that weren't expressly spelled out by your recruiter. Fighting is for matches only; combat away from the cameras comes with serious penalties. Effort must be genuine. A few slick tricksters tried to rig the tournament by throwing matches once, so fake fights are frowned upon. And of course, no quitting once the tournament has begun. Can't imagine that will be a problem since we're down to the final four, but sometimes in the early rounds you get someone who suddenly decided they're in over their head and tries to leave."

"Is that so bad?" Action asked.

The stare Sorsero shot back nearly made him gulp, until it softened moment later. "Right, right, you were looking for clarity. Clearly you haven't been made aware why we're here." Sitting up a bit straighter, Sorsero sucked down a few mouthfuls of green juice, giving his teeth a distracting hue as he explained.

"This whole island is built upon the resting site of something from a long time ago, perhaps another world: the being named Scrabraz. These sites and the beings they hide are peppered around, if you know where to look. His power is what fuels the magical elements of this island, like where our healing resources emanate from, as well as many other tricks you've yet to see. But these resting places are unstable, dangerous, especially if the one sealed isn't properly soothed. Just Scrabraz trying to break free would cause untold havoc. Imagine a tsunami that turned buildings into pudding and people into fish-monsters; that will put you on the right track."

"And a fighting tournament with rocket launchers fixes that?"

Crystalbrawler tapped a dense finger on his metal mug and chuckled. "Well, there *were* rocket launchers in it. I think you're forgetting who won his last match."

"Different places have different methods for the calming the one below." Sorsero looked out the window, to the island and the shoreline, momentarily lost in thought. "This one is soothed by demonstrations of combat, but also enjoys variety. I'd let it go at that, if I were you. Trying to understand magic gives people a migraine, and succeeding leads them even darker places. What matters is that it works, so long as Scrabraz's rules are upheld."

The idea was ludicrous, but no more than werewolves or arm-restoring healing, so Action's mind was more open than it might have normally been. One bit did stand out to him, however. "Hang on, if this is all for the sake of some magical spectator, what's with all the drones and cameras?"

"Food and buildings don't pay for themselves. I said this place was magical, not that it had secret diamond mines." Sorsero polished off his glass of bright green, setting it down on the table with a distinct *click*. "Rich people will spend quite a bit for exclusive entertainment."

A low rumble brought all eyes in the room to Crystalbrawler, who stood from his seat. No wonder he'd been wearing all that padding, half of it was probably to muffle the noise he made. "On the subject of tomorrow's matches, I must retire. The time for revelry has ended, next comes victory, then duty."

He swayed slightly, the effects of the drink still present, but there was still a visible grace to his movements, bulkiness be damned. Sorsero cleared his throat, standing up as well. "I should continue my rounds. There's always more feedback to get." With a pause, Sorsero looked Action up and down once more. "Tell me, have you wondered what happens to those who break our rules, such as attempting to flee?"

"They lose their match?"

"Oh no, they lose quite a bit more than that." Sorsero snapped a finger, and three of the silent workers appeared, seemingly stepping right out of the empty hall. "All who are on this island have agreed to serve the cause once they stepped foot on its soil. Scrabraz doesn't take kindly to those who break their agreement, giving them new roles to fulfill instead. Eventually they're turned free, though many elect to remain. Considering some have been here for hundreds of years, I don't blame them. Whatever world they knew is gone, moved on without them. That's the price for cowardice."

With another snap, the helpers vanished, stepping back into the empty hall they'd arrived from. Sorsero gave Action a large wink before spinning around toward the exit. "I'd recommend you rest up as well, rather than continuing to wander the halls. Tomorrow is going to be a very exciting day."

14

Sleep came in spurts, when Action could doze at all. Stress and fear were battling to keep him conscious, but even in the brief sojourns to the land of slumber, there was no respite to be had. Nightmares were already there waiting for him: visions of Hardy's explosion made more disgusting and blood-filled by imagination, images of Killossus's huge jaws snapping down, even some classics of Pop and Granddad making him drill shuffling until his fingers were worn to literal bones. That last one hadn't been in rotation for many a year, but under pressure like this, there was no telling what might pop out.

Sometime before dawn, he gave up on the notion of sleep, deciding instead to focus on the day ahead. Mindlessly, Action got into a handstand, balanced perfectly, and started knocking out push-ups with the full weight of his body pressing down. For as much his "action-hero" persona was a part of the act, just like the more common varietal of "tuxedoed gentleman" the older generation preferred, he still had to look the part to pull it off. That meant constant exercise and a reasonable eye on his nutrition, though thankfully the tank-top spared Action from needing movie-level abs.

Working out helped clear his mind, drilling down on what his potential moves were. Running was clearly out, and it seemed like throwing a fight could lead to similar circumstances. As things stood, there were only three potential matches left for Action: Tim, Crystalbrawler, and Killossus. Action felt reasonably sure neither Tim nor Crystalbrawler would go for the kill. They hadn't in any prior matches, and there was no reason to suspect they'd want him dead. Killossus, on the other hand, had permanently taken out Bernie Sensation, albeit a bit inadvertently, and might have done the same to Stang if the first bite hadn't gone down so rough. A one-in-three chance of probable survival wasn't great, but it beat the hell out of untold years working here.

That might not be enough, however. If luck wasn't on his side, Action was going to need a backup plan. His eyes wandered over to his trunk, packed with tools and tricks for the magic show he was evidently not here to perform. There might be some options in there, things he could use for quick surprises like the flash-smokes; however, the great majority of it required time to prepare. Something to keep in mind when he knew more about the upcoming battle, though not much help for the time being.

By the time Action's morning routine was done, he felt slightly sore, well-limbered, and unexpectedly relaxed. His course was set, and whether that was for good or ill would bear out over time, but at least he had an idea of what to do with himself. After taking the time to enjoy a long, hot shower, Action dressed for the day, making sure to stuff his over-sized pants with enough tricks that he'd have options, without adding enough weight to slow him down. If the fight with Steven Cage was any indication, speed was going to be Action's friend during all this.

Breakfast was already being served by the time Action arrived, ushered quickly to one of the four chairs at the large table still ready from the night before. At the lesser seats, he saw the other competitors, some looking over with envy, a few with rage, and Steven Cage banged a plate down so hard it made Chef Brunoise jump a few seats over. The former star glared daggers at Action before turning to his high-piled plate.

To his surprise, Action found that Tim wasn't just already present at their big table, he'd begun piling up plates as that huge form downed stacks of pancakes and whole rashers of bacon. "Morning, sleepyhead."

"The sun's barely been risen for half an hour. What time did you get up?" Action's own plate contained mostly lean protein, with a few strips of bacon and one piece of French toast because if he was risking death today, then a few decent meals felt like a fair trade-off.

"No idea, never wear a watch and I couldn't see the stars indoors," Tim replied. "My body is used to a daily schedule. Lumberjack work takes an early riser, have to catch the enchanted trees before they're fully awake, otherwise you're in for a hell of a fight."

Thudding steps jerked most of the room's attention to Killossus, who entered and made a line directly for the buffet, taking a silver platter and piling it high with savory meats. In comparison, Crystalbrawler's arrival made almost no impact as the man helped himself to a croissant and coffee. Seeing them all present, Action began to shovel his own food down faster. As someone with a sense of theatrical timing, he was starting to get a sense for when Sorsero would interrupt—

"Good morning, contenders, both those still in the fight and our already eliminated entrants." Sorsero was unseen once more, voice sounding like it came from the building itself. "Today is the finals of our annual tournament, and what a show it is shaping up to be. For our next round to happen, however, we'll first need to determine opponents. That means it's time to draw some lots. Bring out the board!"

From a side hallway came a huge slab of wood atop rolling wheels, complete with a target painted in what Action dearly hoped was merely cheap red paint. As it moved, more attendants arrived at the table, arms conspicuously laden down with various bladed weapons. Just when Action thought there might be a stabbing fight as warm-up for the next round, Sorsero's voice picked back up on its explanation.

"We like to add a little agency to this one. Throw in whatever order you like, but be aware, whoever's blade you land closest to will be your opponent."

Action's mind flashed to shuffleboard, and while it wasn't a perfect comparison, there were certainly parallels. Whoever went first would be at a disadvantage, since the others would be able to influence how the fights were shaped. Of course, that assumed a throw went exactly as intended. There were always errors to account for.

While he was mulling over the potential implications, someone else was already on the move. Killossus took a hefty cleaver from one of the attendants and hurled it into the huge wooden board, causing a slight split mere inches from the bulls-eye. That done, Killossus went right back to eating, sending the clear message that he didn't care who his opponent would be.

Crystalbrawler stood up next, firing a sparkling shard from his left arm that sank deep into the wood, landing perhaps two-hands-width away from Killossus's still vibrating cleaver. Given how close they were, that made Action's task all the easier. He turned to the workers, eyeing the options before selecting a well-weighted dagger.

It had been many years since he'd done any long-range dagger throwing, not since those days of training in the basement. But the Kadabra family education was not one easily forgotten—some lessons were worn into the bones themselves. As Action stood there, taking aim, it all came flooding back and he let the blade go with near-perfect form. It sailed through the air before landing near the board's right edge, well apart from Killossus and Crystalbrawler.

This was as good as he could hope for. Those two would deal with each other, while he lost to—

The *snap* of a new blade slicing into wood jerked Action out of his reverie, drawing his eye to the still-shaking axe resting mere inches from Killossus's cleaver. The whoop of joy from Action's side made it clear that this was no fluke: Tim had been aiming to get that match-up. The axe hadn't even fully stopped before Sorsero's voice blared out, making the announcement for all to hear.

"Based on the contestants' throwing, it appears our next matches will be Action Kadabra versus Crystalbrawler, and Tim Burly versus Killossus. What a morning we are in for!"

15

In what Action dearly hoped wasn't a sign of things to come, he and Crystalbrawler were assigned Field 4, also known as a graveyard. Well, a graveyard if every single tomb was either a full mausoleum or at least a marble headstone. It was like the ground had sprouted countless dull stone teeth, jutting out at irregular angles. The scene was scary enough, but every time Action looked at Crystalbrawler, his stomach dropped all the more. His was not an expression of someone planning to take this easy.

There was one silver lining Action could cling to: Crystalbrawler didn't have any reason to especially want him dead. Based on the bouts so far, that probably meant Crystalbrawler wouldn't push the fight further than it had to go. On the other hand, everyone here was so strong, and some of the attacks he'd seen others absorb or avoid would have splattered Action like a fresh lasagna dropped on the floor. Crystalbrawler not *meaning* to kill him wouldn't count for a whole lot if Action was still dead. Which meant he was just going to have to find a way to survive.

Drones buzzed overhead, covering the entire field with

their cameras. They seemed louder today; Action wondered if there were more filling the sky, but he dared not look away from his opponent. Any moment now, and it would begin.

"Contestants, we have reached the semi-finals round. Bring your best to bear because everyone you will face today has proven their mettle, and the danger they represent. You third match begins...now!"

On a hunch, Action shot to the side, rolling behind one of the headstones. His instincts were spot-on, as moments later two crystal shards thudded into the ground after passing directly through where he'd been standing. From the angle, it looked as if Crystalbrawler was targeting his legs, but one came in high enough to make Action incredibly thankful he'd dodged that shot. As expected, Crystalbrawler was coming out of the gate hard, trying to end this fast and save his energy for the "true" battle ahead. Action had no objection to losing this fight, he just wanted to do so in a way that didn't result in death or years serving some mysterious magical monster.

Pulling a flash-smoke from one of the many hidden compartments on his pants, Action flicked a hand briefly into view from behind the stone. Seconds later, the telltale tinkle of crystal shattering against the headstone could be heard. Adding another flash-smoke to his free hand, Action threw both at once, fogging both his left and right exit options.

Rather than take either, Action instead crawled forward as more shards peppered the clouds on each side. While Crystalbrawler was distracted, Action slipped behind a new tombstone farther back, pausing momentarily for a long breath. He couldn't afford to start panting and potentially give away his position. In this battle, surprise might well be the only element that even *could* work in his favor.

Listening for Crystalbrawler's movements, hoping to slip

around and perhaps score a few sneaky hits before inevitable defeat, Action realized that the drone noise was only getting worse. In fact, the thundering whirr was starting to sound much too loud for such small devices. Chancing a peek up to the sky, Action could see something farther in the distance, an object closing at rapid speed.

A sudden crashing sound brought him back to the battle, where Crystalbrawler had just ripped Action's original hiding headstone out of the ground and tossed it aside. Evidently, he was getting sick of the ranged attacks, opting for a more expedient method. It would only be moments until Action was discovered if he didn't act quickly.

Growing up, Action had never understood why his Granddad insisted on drilling fundamentals so constantly, especially for tricks that had long fallen out of vogue. But the old magician had merely shaken his head at the young student and said, "What I'm giving you are tools. The jobs they serve may change, but it's handy to have them around. The more tools you're equipped with, the more options are at hand when shit hits the fan."

"Hey, big fella, what's wrong, got rocks in your eyes, or you just too stoned to see me slip past?"

While the words originated from Action, they seemed to echo from behind Crystalbrawler, as though his adversary had snuck around unseen at some point in battle. Throwing one's voice wasn't a trick many magicians bothered with anymore, largely leaving it to those specialized in ventriloquism. But Granddad believed the power to make people look where he wanted was one of the greatest skills a magician could master, and every skill serving that goal was deemed worthy of passing on.

"The hell did you get by?" Crystalbrawler turned, annoyance tangible in his voice. Action realized that perhaps annoying him mid-fight might not play out so great when he was eventually caught, but before he could call out, Crystalbrawler's voice continued. "And what the hell is that racket?"

True enough, the noise was undeniable now, and Action chanced peeking out from behind his stone to see a helicopter hovering above the drones. It was familiar, and he quickly realized this was the same vehicle that had ascended during their mercenary skirmish near the boat, the one Steven Cage was piloting.

"You think you can embarrass me like that?" It was indeed Steven Cage's voice that blared from the speaker, half-strangled with madness but recognizable all the same. "It's starting those terrible rumors all over again! Well not this time. I worked too hard, spent too much money to win back my pride. Come on out, Action Kadabra, and let me show you my ultimate technique. It'll make Rocket Launcher Dave look like Roman Candl— Shit!"

Jerking the controls, Steven's helicopter tried to swerve away from the crystal shards striking at the exterior, one embedding itself deep into the windshield. Crystalbrawler had both hands up and was continuing to fire, only pausing to adjust his aim. "Nobody interrupts my fights."

"Stop shooting! I'm going to hand you victory." Steven's voice crackled out from the helicopter sound system, unable to hear Crystalbrawler's softly spoken words. When more projectiles came, his tone turned venomous. "Fine! You can lose together."

That was all the warning Action needed. Trusting both men to be distracted, he hopped to his feet and began to sprint. Not too far off was a mausoleum, one with thick stone walls and matching doors already standing slightly ajar. Leaping through the opening, Action paused only long enough to throw his entire shoulder against the door, ample muscles working hard to hurriedly force it closed. With that done, he scanned the room, searching for any additional protection.

Less than a minute later, Steven Cage finally managed to get the weapons systems armed and operational, sparing less than a second of thought before he opened fire. Two missiles shot forth, one aimed at the graveyard as a whole, the other directly centered on Crystalbrawler.

Huge explosions rocked the graveyard, seemingly reducing the entire field and both competitors to nothing more than rubble.

16

The thudding of the helicopter blades slicing the air could still be faintly heard overhead as Action shifted the heavy stone lid, surprised to see sunshine glaring down at him. The roof of the mausoleum, along with most of the mausoleum itself, was in ruins. So was the vast majority of the battlefield, as Action's eyes swept the carnage.

What had once been a graveyard was now a sheen of total destruction. Shattered tombstones littered the ground like a dark marble sand, small fires had caught in the brush, and at impact points where the missiles hit, one could see the beginnings of coffins peeking out of the ground. Suppressing a shudder, Action tried not to think about what might be inside. Luck had been with him when he chose an empty tomb to take cover in, and he wasn't looking to press his fortune on that front.

He finished climbing from the stone box, thick lid and walls being an extra layer of protection that turned out to be quite well chosen. Action's eyes continually flashed to the sky, too aware of the helicopter noise still somewhere nearby. Steven was probably doing a sweep, making sure there were no survivors.

A new noise grabbed Action's attention, the sound of coughing. No way... there was no way someone could have survived that, not even Crystalbrawler. Right? Not trusting what should or shouldn't be impossible on this island, Action changed directions, heading toward the noise. For a moment, he thought it might have been imagined, before noticing the edges of an impact crater that was masked by dirt and debris. Setting his hands to digging, Action pawed through the dirt, hurling it aside, pausing only when the helicopter's noise grew noticeably louder.

Just when it seemed like the cough might have been in his mind, the ground sprang to life, one of Crystalbrawler's hands shooting out and groping for freedom. Quickly, Action grabbed it, digging his feet in to act as an anchor while they both pulled. The dirt nearby suddenly sank in as Crystalbrawler tore his way to freedom, bursting into the air and coughing up huge clumps of dirt.

It was almost hard to recognize Crystalbrawler, a huge amount of his eponymous crystals were gone, only the sections closest to his skin still intact. He looked more human, and frail, that Action could have imagined moments prior. Shakily, Crystalbrawler tried to rise to his feet, only to crash back down moments later. Surviving a missile barrage might be in his capabilities, but it wasn't a trick that left him unscathed.

Action tried to help him up, all the more enthusiastically as he noticed the volume of the helicopter increasing once more. Together, they made it a few steps before Crystalbrawler stumbled yet again. The wounded competitor spat out a harsh, pained laugh. "All this work, just to die here, by some idiot with an arsenal. Two years in a row I've fallen short."

"It's not over yet," Action urged, trying to pull him farther along. Eventually, they could reach trees or undecimated sections of the graveyard, either would offer more cover than their current position.

"You don't quite get how this contest works, do you?" Crystalbrawler tried to release another laugh, but instead he devolved into a coughing fit and spit up more dirt. "This is when you strike the winning blow and move on."

That wasn't a terrible idea, had Action *wanted* to keep fighting. As things stood, he was hoping the interference would make this whole match get thrown out. A bit of a fantasy, but in his predicament, one sought comfort where they could. Still, he had to play the part. Sorsero and all the others were watching, Scrabraz presumably included.

"Did you come to this tournament to prove you could score an easy hit on an opponent someone else wounded, or did you come to prove you were the best?" Action threw a shoulder under Crystalbrawler's ribs, half-hauling him to his feet. "Survive our interruption, get healed, and then we can put on a match worthy of this event."

"Hmmph." The grunt from Crystalbrawler wasn't especially enthusiastic, though he did try to put more weight on his legs. "You may not possess the keenest mind for victory, but I respect the integrity with which you fight."

A nice sentiment Action dearly hoped he remembered if they *did* have to step back in a ring together. Noise caught his ear, and Crystalbrawler tilted his head as well, staring up at the sky.

"Not that what either of us does matters. It sounds like he's circling back around."

That was Action's assessment as well, which was why he started to double-time it across the scorched ground. Where they were headed, he had no idea, but if he kept going in one direction, there was bound to be something eventually. He pressed on as the airborne blades grew more distinct, all-but dragging Crystalbrawler each step of the way. As the sound grew louder, the pointlessness of it was driven home; however, Action refused to quit.

"Enough." Crystalbrawler jerked away without warning, swaying on his feet, but ultimately managing to stand. "This isn't going to work. Only one of us is still mobile enough to stand a chance. Go. I'll distract him and buy you more time."

"You don't need to do that," Action protested. He couldn't let this man get drawn into his and Steven's strange feud.

Crystalbrawler shook his head. "We all fight our own way. You save people you should beat; I refuse to back down even against impossible odds. Now go. I owe that piece of shit some payback."

Just as Action was about to turn, the helicopter came into view. It was wobbling about in the sky now, Steven's control must be slipping, but jerked directly toward them the instant it had line-of-sight. Despite knowing he had to go, Action stood there, feet momentarily frozen by the insanity of it all.

That feeling increased exponentially moments later, when the ground began to shake. Huge cracks suddenly appeared in the graveyard, near where Action had hidden in his mausoleum. From the deepest of them came a huge lash of flame, stretching high into the sky and wrapping around the helicopter even as it tried to dodge. The fire-lash went taught, then began to wind in, yanking the vehicle and pilot down together.

Just as Steven passed by ground-level, Action was able to catch sight of him through the cockpit window. He had no idea what Steven Cage was looking at, only that his gaze was angled downward, and the man was screaming like someone who might keel over from fright.

Fast as it started, the shaking halted and the cracks sealed back up, like they'd never been there. Nearby, Crystalbrawler managed a very short "Oh thank the Great Shard" before keeling over onto his back, no longer able to stand.

Even though he knew it was coming, Action still winced at the sound of Sorsero's voice. "Since Crystalbrawler is no longer able to fight and Steven Cage has been taken by Scrabraz for match interference, that makes the winner of our semi-final matchup to be...Action Kadabra! With the other fight already concluded, that means he'll be facing Killossus in the Final Round!"

ction barely paid attention as he was led by the silent workers down the winding path, over the hills of multi-colored grass, and through the forest of flickering shadows. It wasn't until they were passing into the Hallowed Hall that he noticed a new route was being taken, one he hadn't seen before. In fact, he was almost certain that until now, this hallway had led to a dead end.

Well, the hallway was certainly thriving now. Huge banners of various hues hung along the gold-trimmed walls, leading to a massive set of doors waiting at the end, like a pristine, yet hungry, mouth. Action plodded along, only peripherally realizing that the other forms had fallen away as his trek began. With only his footsteps echoing from the polished marble, it was a lonely, almost haunting walk.

No sooner had Action stepped through the doors than he realized how short-lived such a feeling would be. Massive stands lined the walls, enough to fit hundreds, perhaps even more with whatever magics this place had available. Were these a relic of times gone by? Perhaps, but they looked quite well maintained. Between context clues and a general hunch in his gut, Action had a feeling their last bout would be in front of a crowd.

Once his eyes slid from the stands, he was able to properly take in the area where they'd be fighting. It was plain, especially compared to the luxury of the cushions and silks decorating the stands. Nothing more than a slightly raised platform, three feet off the ground and made of pale stone. Reaching forward, Action rubbed his hands against the rough surface, getting a feel for the texture. Certain moves required traction; others depended on the capability to slide. Action didn't have a plan in mind, he was still largely numb from the bizarre experience he'd just survived. But it seemed prudent to know what his most effective way to dodge those hideous chomping jaws would be.

"Really thought I might get a chance to fight in here." The voice took him by surprise; however, it was a friendly, familiar one. Action turned to find Stang walking over, sipping on a large milkshake. His semi-human arm was looking more in line with the rest of him, thick purple veins swelling all the way down to his wrists. "Not my year, but at least I've got someone to cheer for."

"Any word on Tim?" Part of Action was afraid to ask. The silent workers had been no help, and he had no idea where anyone else was though, so he couldn't miss the opportunity.

"Torn up to hell, but still kicking with the leg he had left," Stang replied. "Didn't go down easy, either. He and Killossus are both receiving some deep healing, think I saw Crystalbrawler getting attention too. You're the only one to get out of Round Three undamaged."

Given the amount of psychological trauma this trip had entailed, Action wasn't sure he'd call himself "undamaged," but it was hard to argue on the physical front. So far, luck and quick reflexes had kept him afloat. Unfortunately, the former appeared to have run out. No matter how Action looked at the next arena, he was screwed.

Every tactic he'd used so far was about speed and dexterity, neither of which would be applicable in a setting like this. Sure, maybe if he was supernatural-fighter-fast or had cheetah legs or something else to fit in with this crowd, it might be enough to make a difference. As things stood, however, there was little hope to grasp for. Flat, open space exposed every angle to the crowd. Nowhere to hide, nowhere to run. Action might as well be trying to fight someone in the middle of a stage.

The notion sparked something in Action's mind, a mad notion, visions of a trick his Grandad had taught him so many years ago. It was an idea ridiculous enough to be easily dismissed on any other day. But here, standing before a platform where he was to fight to the near-death, after days of madness and seeing some underground monster lasso a helicopter out of the sky, there *were* no bad ideas. Good and bad quality were concepts like sanity and reality: they had little purpose or use on Scrabraz Island. Senseless as his idea might be, it was persistent, and the more it clanged around his skull, the more Action began to take it seriously.

Sorsero had been abundantly clear that the battlefields were fair game before the match started. If Steven Cage could stick bombs under the sand, then Action felt within his rights to add a bit of dramatic flair. Maybe even a little more, at that. He might not have all of his props or equipment, but he had the essentials locked away in his trunk.

"How long until the next match?" Action was looking at the room once more, no longer with defeat in his eyes. The odds of this working, or even making a difference in the slightest, were infinitesimal. Like the chances of shuffling a deck of cards into exactly the order one wanted. But then, what *was* magic, if not finding a way to make the impossible seem real?

There were some loud sucking sounds as Stang finished up the last of his shake. "Few hours until the crowds arrive, at least. Final bout is always in the evening, that way there's time to get the combatants fully healed up and ready. It's the last scheduled event of the night, so everyone has to be in top condition for a grand finale."

He had time to work with, but was it enough? Action's mind was whirring, picturing different set-ups and combinations, discarding and refining as fast as they appeared. Generations worth of magician's knowledge and skill were packed into Action all his life, there might be a great many areas where he would fall short, but the art of illusion was always the exception.

"I think I've got work to do," Action announced.

"Want some help?" Stang set the empty shake glass down on a counter, where it was whisked away by a silent worker seemingly stepping from the shadows.

Much as he would love the extra hands, Action had just seen what happened to rule breakers. "Is that allowed?"

"Sure. I lost, I'm out of the tournament, so as far as anyone here is concerned, I'm just a spectator. I might not be able to join the fight, but I'm free to help whoever I want prepare. Between my drinking buddy and the guy who tore off my arm, guess who I'm rooting for?"

That settled it then. Action had time, opportunity, and now even additional manpower. He had to at least *try.* The Kadabra pride he'd inherited would allow for nothing else.

"Then first off, I need you to go find me every mirror you think won't be missed, all the banners you can easily reach, and every scrap of rope on this island that can be spared."

Looking over the room with a forming vision, Action grinned like he hadn't since setting foot on the island.

"Time to show them how a man of magic does battle."

1 8

No more silent arena, not this time. Action stood in the wings, attended by several of the silent workers, as he waited for the cue to come. His lower back and arms were sore. Hastily assembling most of an act out of sight took a toll on even Action's toned body. Leaning slightly forward, he peeked out from behind the wall shielding him, at the massive number of bodies filling every last seat of the stands. It was, without question, the largest audience Action had ever gotten the chance to step in front of. Hell, this rivaled the greatest crowds Pop ever managed to pull in. He wondered if Granddad and Pop would be proud that this many people would see the Kadabra art in person, but deep down Action suspected so long as he clung to his current moniker and stage persona, there was no amount of success that could change their minds. They believed in the classics, but he wanted to push the envelope and try new things.

Then again, look at where being open to new experiences had gotten him. Maybe those old geezers had a point.

"Good evening all, and welcome to the final round of this year's tournament!" Sorsero's voice almost sounded odd, hearing it in person rather than blaring out from drone speakers. It was drowned out moments later by thunderous applause, all of which cut off at once, likely due to some gesture from the stage. "The rules are simple, yet unyielding. The first competitor to die, quit, be rendered helpless, or leave the arena by their own power loses the match. I know you've all been waiting eagerly for this moment, so let's not delay. Bring forth the competitors!"

A nod from one of the workers was all Action needed. He stepped out into view without delay. Pausing for a moment, he basked in the attention, aware of every eye taking him in. From the spikey hair, to the worn tank-top showing off his honed physique, to the over-sized parachute style pants that had long been out of fashion. True to his name, Action looked like he'd stepped off the set of a film filled with cheap gun fights and too many explosions. There were whispers of curiosity, and doubt, especially once Killossus appeared.

They cheered the huge creature as he thudded his way along the floor, approaching the raised platform where Sorsero was already waiting. Whatever damage Tim had done was long-gone. Killossus looked fresh and ready for battle, going so far as to lick his snout when he and Action made eye-contact. A nice psych-out, but the upshot of being brain-scrambling terrified was that Action couldn't really get *more* scared.

Stepping onto the platform, both competitors approached Sorsero, who was holding a huge book, the spine of it longer than Action's forearm. As they drew closer, the book parted, opening to reveal two blank pages formed from what looked like gold. Looking to each of them, Sorsero spoke with the most somber tone that Action had heard so far.

"Before you begin, you must speak your names. Your *real* names, not the titles worn here. Getting to this point was mere preamble. This is a sacred ceremony with magics to be followed. Say your name, accept your role as competitor, and we shall appease Scrabraz for another year."

"Killaby MacDonald." The words caused Action to jump. Hearing Killossus speak was already jarring, all the more so when he was pronouncing a mouthful of a name like that one. Seconds later, golden lines appeared on one of the blank pages, weaving together in a script that almost looked like a name, yet not quite.

It had been a long time since Action spoke his true name, and the streak would have continued under other circumstances. But he hadn't survived this long to get swallowed by the ground over a technicality, even if the words did sting as they passed his lips. "Abraham Kadabra, the Third."

Sorsero's eyes narrowed slightly as the golden writing appeared once more, the mental wheels already spinning. "Wouldn't that make your name—"

"Abra-Kadabra, the Third" Action confirmed. "Granddad changed it when he got into the business and decided the name was so good he wanted to pass it along."

A short snicker and a shake-of-the-head from Sorsero. "No wonder you have something to prove." He slammed the book shut, nodding to each. "Introduce yourselves and your styles to the crowd, and then I will call to begin."

While Sorsero was walking off, Killossus turned to the audience, letting out a roar that nearly shook the drinks in their hands. Only when he was done, and every eye in the room was on him, did Killossus deign to grunt a few syllables. "Killossus. Decimation-style."

"Good evening, all you wonderful people, how's my audience tonight?" Action lifted his hands, gesturing for some sort of reaction, perhaps even applause, but instead was treated to near silence. He pressed on without a hitch. If playing to unreceptive viewers was enough to shake Action, he'd have failed out of his career years ago. "Outstanding! Well my name is Action Kadabra, and I am here to show off my own unique style of combat: Illusion-style."

Just as Action was winding up for more patter, Sorsero's voice called from the sidelines. "Begin!"

There was barely even a moment to react. Killossus was moving the instant he could. A huge swing of his clawed hand came crashing down, slashing against the ground where Action had been a mere instant before. Only endless years of reflex training and stage-awareness allowed Action to nimbly dodge, and even then, it was close.

If Action had a hope of winning, he had to come out of the gates swinging as well. From a concealed sheath inside his voluminous pants, Action produced a throwing dagger. This one was custom made, built to resemble something more tactical than the weighted model people typically associated with blade-throwers, an aesthetic that went with his action-star persona and act as a whole.

Killossus didn't appear to be worried by the newly produced blade, lunging for Action with a mighty clamp of those tremendous jaws. They closed with such force Action could swear he felt a gust of wind. Backpedaling fast, he shifted the blade in his hand, trying desperately to line-up the right shot. There *were* backups on him, but those had their own purpose, and besides this was the one Action used most often in his act. The throws after this would only get harder.

Recovering from his last lunge, Killossus spun around just in time to see Action with the blade raised high and his arm pulled back, a toss eminent. In one motion, the monster of a man dropped low as he surged forward, grabbing for Action's legs. The blade left Action's hand, but sailed directly over Killossus's head, striking somewhere against the far wall.

No blade to defend with, and no room to run. Killossus grinned, a smile that morphed into an open mouth, ready to devour his prey.

19

Whistling filled the air as objects dropped from the ceiling, one nearly bashing Killossus on the head as it plummeted, halting only moments before impact against the ground. The inhuman competitor whirled around, searching for his prey, but was confronted only by banners and mirrors that had plainly been stolen from around the island and hung up on a series of suspended cables.

Cables that had all been held by a single anchor point, the now-sundered rope where Action's dagger could be seen on the lying nearby. What had looked like a wild throw to those in attendance was in fact merely the opening of Action's true performance.

It had taken quite a while to get this prepared, mimicking the setup as close to what Action remembered as possible. The Teleporting Magician was an illusion originally developed for theatre-in-the-round, a trick that would be impressive no matter the viewer's angle. Between the cloths and the mirrors, Action should be able to seemingly appear and vanish, weaving between the carefully hidden gaps amidst the obfuscation. Whether it would be enough to win his survival would have to be seen; however, at least he was no longer in open view.

"My audience, it is my great pleasure to welcome you to a once in a lifetime event: a chance to experience the magic of action!" As the magician moved, throwing his voice to keep his true location unknown, he worked his way around the platform, stopped at each of the descended mirrors. More than merely a way to confuse his opponent, they also made a handy way to stash his more cumbersome gear.

Killossus slashed at a banner, nearly getting tangled up for his troubles, as Action stepped into position, dropping several small devices at his feet from the left hand while pulling a tremendously over-sized gun in his right. It was closer to a cannon honestly, the sort of ridiculous firearm that only proved useful in highly specialized circumstances and action movies. "As always, these things tend to start with gunplay."

To Killossus, it was as if Action had stepped from nowhere. While all of this clutter was distracting for him, Action was effectively in his home turf, well used to nimble, concealed movements. Usually he had to hide from an entire crowd; in comparison, one toothy fighter wasn't nearly as challenging. With as much grandiosity as possible, Action took aim, making sure Killossus had plenty of time to see him and dodge.

Instead, Killossus let out a hideous snarl and bolted forward, eyes only on the target before him. Jaws came snapping down, shattering the mirror-version of Action and carving up the top of Killossus's mouth something awful. At the side of his temple, the real gun came into view inches away, visible for only an instant before Action pulled the trigger.

Sparks shot out, one rogue fleck landing near Killossus's

left eye, causing him to jerk away in reflex. Action raised the gun overhead, aiming carefully away from the banners, where it fired a miniature firework into the ceiling, causing a momentary flash during which Action scattered more small devices.

"Don't worry folks, we're not here to put on some hurried display. Guns might be more efficient, but they're much too boring, especially when we have people here to see a *show!*" Also, Action didn't *have* a real gun to use. This whole plan was made of props and techniques intended for soothing drunk gamblers, so some tools were going to have to fill new roles.

A smattering of applause rippled forth, along with a soft undercurrent of laughter at the spooked Killossus. He seemed to be aware of it, eyes narrowing and whipping toward the crowd. While it did momentarily quiet the snickers, Action recognized that move for the rookie mistake it was. Cowing the audience into silence wouldn't make things better; he'd still know they were laughing, and now that was all he'd likely hear. One didn't defeat an audience through fear, but rather through winning them over.

Before Killossus could recover, Action was gone, disappeared into the mirrors and banners once more, save for his voice. "Seems my agitated assistant didn't enjoy that last trick too much. Don't worry, the next one will be much more up his alley. I bet the sharp ones among you can even guess where we're heading next." More patter to soothe the audience and rile Killossus. Sounds of breaking glass rang out, seemed Killossus had finally hit on the solution of smashing the mirrors.

Grabbing more of the small devices from the back of a mirror, Action also picked up a coil of steel wire and a specialty prop knife. There was a good chance he wouldn't have enough time for another refill, not at the rate those scaley fists could break reflective surfaces. Hunkering down, Action scattered a few devices, then hooked a premade loop in the steel wire to a screw-eye he'd lodged in the mirror's frame. In seconds he was back up, dashing along, leaving a generous trail of steel wire behind.

Stepping momentarily into view, Action hurled another of his throwing knives toward Killossus. It did little, merely nicking a shoulder, but that was enough to draw instant attention. Now sure of a real target, Killossus hurled himself across the platform, slamming down into open air and letting out a roar of frustration. Laughter rang out from the crowd, along with some short cheers. They were having fun, which only angered Killossus more.

For nearly a full minute, they played out the dance: Action moving around the field, hitting him with a dagger, then vanishing before there was a chance for rebuttal. Until, inevitably, Action was almost out of real knives. All he had left was the specialty prop knife and one more actual dagger. Checking his pockets to be sure there were no devices left to scatter, Action confirmed the prep work was done. Time to see if he could pull off this trick or not.

When Action came into view this time, he was closer to Killossus. Too close, to those watching from the stands, as a hideous gasp bloomed in the crowd. Whirled around, Killossus sprang, jaws open for a brief moment before slamming down. What they crashed upon was not Action's hand as hoped, however, but merely the knife. That might not have been so bad, especially since he was already ignoring mouth wounds, except it wasn't *just* a knife. Something in his mouth expanded, and Killossus fell to the ground, choking. From his snout drifted a plastic petal, the kind one might find on a fake bouquet that sprang out of a prop weapon.

Choking him with the prop might have been a good plan but didn't take into account Killossus's capacity to empty his gullet. The bouquet came gushing out, along with several pounds of food and what looked like Stang's finger. Spinning around, Killossus found himself looking across the platform to Action, who was half-facing the crowd.

"Much as I would love to entertain you all day, I fear my assistant's patience is running short. Let's wrap up the way all great action battles do: with gratuitous amounts of needless fire." Flicking a button on a small remote, Action activated the dozens of small devices he'd been seeding along the ground. Each one produced a sizable spurt of flame, tapering down slightly after the initial flare. The diminished long-term performance was irrelevant, because they'd already accomplished their true job.

The hanging banners thought to be no more than extra obfuscation all caught light instantly, as if they'd been treated in some sort of specialty magician-developed accelerant, an investment that had taken all of Action's stores and a good deal of time but was providing undeniable dividends in the form of a shocked, perhaps even scared, Killossus.

The showman in Action knew to capitalize on moments like this when he had them, so with Killossus momentarily cowed, Action tilted his eyes toward the crowd and gestured toward the platform all but filled with fire.

"Now then, who wants to see the magic of action?"

For the first time in a very, *very* long while, Action Kadabra felt the surge that came from an audience's cheers. Pleasant as it was, he also didn't dare bask for long. Shows weren't remembered for or determined by their middle game.

Time to try for one hell of a finale.

Between all the missed strikes, the turning of the crowd, and now fire seeming to drip down from the ceiling, Killossus was unquestionably off his game as he scrambled back, searching for a safe place within the growing inferno. Action, on the other hand, was racing around the arena seemingly without concern, perhaps because of the flame-retardant gel covering his exposed skin and hair. For someone whose act frequently featured fire, it was an absolute necessity to keep on hand.

Scary as the fire might be though, its purpose wasn't to win the fight. There was no way to turn the searing surroundings offensive without putting himself equally at risk, and it was only a matter of time until they burned out. No, these were merely part of the grander plan, another cog in the great machine magicians depended on above all others: these were for misdirection.

As Killossus struggled to recover, Action's worked continued, looping to steel wiring around the remaining screws set in the mirrors. Right as the fire was starting to wane, Action looped the last hook and snared a quick breath.

Everything up until now had been about avoidance and controlling the battlefield. But there was no getting around the next part if he hoped to snare victory: Action had to go on the attack.

Circling around the rear, Action's steps were less than a whisper as he crept up to Killossus, the huge scaly man's attention occupied by the scraps of falling fabric raining atop his head. He snapped at them, rearing up to try and rip away a section of banner, and presenting Action with exactly the chance he'd been hoping for.

With dexterity and speed honed by literal countless hours of practice, Action's hands sprang into action. He slipped the end of the wire through a metal gripping mechanism and locked it in place, then whipped the whole thing around Killossus's thick neck, encircling the flesh completely before Action caught his gripping section once more. The instant Killossus felt pressure, he started to twist around, but before he could finish the rotation, Action yanked on the wire, visibly digging into Killossus's neck.

The pain caused him to hesitate, which gave Action a chance to drop low and whip the end of the wire around Killossus's left ankle, springing up and ensnaring his right forearm. Another jerk of the wire, and this time it sent Killossus sprawling to the ground thanks to a lack of balance. In the brief moment on his back, Killossus found the wire being speedily wrapped around his limbs, binding him further.

Overhead, the banners were beginning to die out, offering the crowd a clear view of Action standing atop his momentarily bested foe. Even this, Killossus would probably manage to break out of, between his strength and durability, capture had always been impossible. Reaching into his pants, Action pulled free his final knife, one saved for a very special purpose.

"I've never intentionally killed someone before," Action admitted, these words softer than the others, though not hidden from the crowd. His eyes strayed to the seating near the front, where fellow competitors were watching. Crystalbrawler was looking back and offered a solemn nod to the unspoken question. "But if I have to break that record, at least this is one I can feel okay about. Whatever bits of humanity are left in there, please don't worry. I'm setting you free."

Action lifted the blade high overhead, aim set for Killossus's exposed neck. All that stopped him from jabbing down was the sudden look of terror in his captive's eyes, paired with a sudden verbal objection.

"Whoa, wait, what the fuck?" Killossus, displaying more articulation than previously demonstrated, suddenly started sputtering out words at a desperate speed. "I don't want to die! You think because I'm a lizard-creature I'd be burning to croak? This shit rules. I'm huge, strong, and can eat whatever I want without caring about calories."

Knife still overhead, Action's hand hesitated. When he'd been certain this was a mercy, it has still been a tough choice to make. Now that there was doubt, the idea of slitting a throat was starting to seem a lot more extreme than moment prior. "But... Crystalbrawler said you were—"

"Yeah, *that's* the guy who needs to be set free," Killossus said, agreeing with a very different point than Action was leading to. "Half of why I came to this thing was to give my old friend some peace from whatever hell he's living in."

From the audience, a familiar voice rang out. "Screw you! I love my rock powers. You're the one who looks like a rejected Ninja Turtles villain."

"At least I'm still biological, meaning I've got my dick." Killossus was struggling against the wire still, though now it was more to try and get a better vantage on Crystalbrawler. "I bet you're pissing out of a rock-candy stick."

With a single clap, the room fell silent. Sorsero stepped into view, a spotlight shining down instantly from somewhere unseen. As someone who'd been crawling around the ceiling and knew there was no lighting equipment up there, Action was extra impressed. Moving deliberately, Sorsero stepped up onto the elevated platform that was their battlefield. Each step clacked off the hard stone as he moved, until at last he stood between Action and Killossus.

"It is rare, quite rare, that this particular match does not end in death. By this point, the combatants who have reached the final round often will settle only for victory of demise, forcing such a point. However, the true purpose of this event is entertainment, and on that front, I feel this year's match has been a *rousing* success. Killossus seems to have been rendered helpless, and Action has elected to spare his life. What say you, audience?"

Cheers screamed forth like they'd been waiting for a chance to slip off the tongue. Action basked in them, all too aware that his life might take a terrible turn in the next few moments, determined to enjoy the experience while he could. After nearly a full minute, Sorsero motioned for silence, and received it.

"Very well. As overseer of this tournament, it is my pleasure to announce that our winner for this round is Action Kadabra, wielding Illusion-style." This time the audience broke out into full-on celebration. Someone else might have described it as pandemonium, but to a man accustomed to dealing with gambling drunks in the middle of the night, it was merely hectic.

Still, there was enough noise that no one else could possibly hear Sorsero as he lifted Action's hand and pulled him in close. "Congratulations on your victory, and prize money. Might I suggest putting some of that toward training. When the final match is won without killing, it signifies the victor to be of exceptional skill and strength. By tradition, those champions are expected to come back and defend their titles the following year."

Action felt the blood rush from his face, even as he searched Sorsero's face for some sign of falsehood. "Please tell me you're joking."

"Not at all. You're free to try and skip out, though Scrabraz might take it personally."

For an instant, Action felt the ground shake. Looking around, there was no change on anyone else's faces, meaning he was likely the only person to feel it. A direct reminder from whatever lived beneath this island of what happened to those who didn't follow the rules.

"You couldn't have told me that before I spared him?" While he doubted anything would have changed, Action felt well within his rights to do some grumbling.

"Less fun that way. Plus, I was hoping you'd come back. This is one of the best tournaments we've had since the last time a magician got roped into participating."

Action's eyes narrowed, somehow this, *this* was a step too far. "Wait, you knew? And this has happened before?"

With a stage-worthy grin, Sorsero snapped his fingers, producing a single red rose with a trimmed stem. He tucked it into the top left strap of Action's tank top, patting the flower once to be sure it stayed in place.

"Make sure you prepare well, Action Kadabra. Beginner's luck only works the first time, and we're looking forward to another excellent show next year."

As Action whipped across the stage, doing handsprings one after another, the swinging blades flashed ineffectively, always coming within inches of slicing his flesh without ever quite managing to seal the deal. From the crowd, there was scattered applause, along with a long snort from a very drunk gentleman lounging in the corner. He gulped deeply from his glass of cheap brown liquor, then lifted a hand to his mouth.

"Faaaake. You could at least use real blades in this sad little ac—"

The voice suddenly went quiet as a hand-axe lodged itself into his table, so close to his drink-holding hand that it had sliced his sleeve. Now terrified, his intoxicated eyes peered up to the stage, where a face so hairy it was mostly eyes was poking out from behind the curtains. This seemed an excellent cue to mind his own business. At the very least he wasn't going to call into question how real any of this act's blades were again.

"Thank you, everyone!" Action announced after a spinning flip through the air, narrowly avoiding a final flurry of blades. "I am Action Kadabra, and we are so excited you're here to see The Death Island Players. Next up, please enjoy the axe-throwing talents of Tim Burly, master of Lumber-jack-style."

Slipping off the stage, Action threw Tim a nod of thanks for the off-stage assist. Their new act had only been going for a couple of weeks, but already things were changing. More crowds, a bit of buzz, even some cash flowing in from ticket sales. Expanding the show had definitely broadened their appeal, especially with how unique the cast was. Beyond that, however, Action noticed something else was different. Whether it was the joy of collaboration or simply appreci-ating someone having his back, Action was enjoying the stage more than he had in a great while.

One day, maybe he would invite the elder Kadabras to come see what the family screw-up had accomplished, after the act was fully polished. That would have to be a goal for a future performance, however, as Action currently had far too many plates spinning in the air already.

Moving farther backstage, Action passed Stang, who was easily slipping out of a pair of handcuffs thanks to his skin's natural gooeyness. With time, the man might make a hell of an escape artist—he was already learning at a brisk rate. Action kept going, through the dressing area and into the training room.

Aside from paying for upgrades to the act, Action's largest purchase was the building in which they were currently performing. It butted up to an Off-Strip casino, rather than being part of one, which made the cost far more manageable. A good thing, too, since there was one major renovation that had to be undertaken. Building the training room hadn't been cheap; from the huge amount of space, to the array of usable weapons, to the raised section in the middle of the room perfectly matching the one on Scrabraz Island.

On that very platform, Killossus was pinning Crystalbrawler, the latter of whom had nearly regrown all of his stony covering. At Action's arrival, he scrambled up, all focus shifted. It was curious, despite the fact that he hadn't thrown a punch all tournament, the magician had somehow managed to earn his opponents' respect, with maybe even a dash of fear mixed in.

"Okay guys, between set-up and the actual throwing, we've got around twenty minutes until I have to get back out there. Who has the energy for a quick sparring session before you two do the closer?"

"I'll take this one," Crystalbrawler said, climbing to his feet. "You're starting to learn Killossus's timing. Can't go getting comfortable with one opponent. Plus, he needs to practice the choreography for our finale more. We appreciate you giving us a place to stay, so we want to make the show as good as it can be."

Action had been a bit surprised when he talked to the others after the tournament and realized how few of them had any plans for what came next. To most of them, the event had been a place to win, or perish trying. Returning as failures didn't seem to be an option for several, while others simply had no idea where to go. When Action proposed merging their talents, it had largely been idle speculation, but he wasn't going to argue with results.

As things stood, he currently had ten months and two weeks until the next tournament on Scrabraz Island. Climbing up onto the platform, Action let his nimble hands take on the form of fists, squaring off across from Crystalbrawler. Illusions alone might not be enough next time. Action's best and only hope was to expand his bag of tricks, both literally and metaphorically.

The two men rushed toward one another, fists raised, just as the sound of an axe splitting metal echoed from the stage like the ringing of a bell.

ABOUT THE AUTHOR

Drew Hayes is an author from Texas who has now found time and gumption to publish several books. He graduated from Texas Tech with a B.A. in English, because evidently he's not familiar with what the term "employable" means. Drew has been called one of the most profound, prolific, and talented authors of his generation, but a table full of drunks will say almost anything when offered a round of free shots. Drew feels kind of like a D-bag writing about himself in the third person like this. He does appreciate that you're still reading, though.

Drew would like to sit down and have a beer with you. Or a cocktail. He's not here to judge your preferences. Drew is terrible at being serious, and has no real idea what a snippet biography is meant to convey anyway. Drew thinks you are awesome just the way you are. That part, he meant. You can reach Drew with questions or movie offers at Novelist-Drew@gmail.com Drew is off to go high-five random people, because who doesn't love a good high-five? No one, that's who.

Read or purchase more of his work at his site: Drew-HayesNovels.com

ACKNOWLEDGMENTS

Special thanks to Melissa McArthur and Clicking Keys for her editorial help, and John Luther Davis for his amazing cover.